A QUESTION OF HONOR

by

Karen Blake

FAWCETT COVENTRY • NEW YORK

A QUESTION OF HONOR

Published by Fawcett Coventry Books, a unit of CBS Publications, the Consumer Publishing Division of CBS Inc.

ISBN: 0-449-50184-1

Printed in the United States of America

First Fawcett Coventry printing: May 1981

10   9   8   7   6   5   4   3   2   1

One

CHIVALRY: The attitude of a man toward a strange woman.

Anonymous

1816

Kate leaned back wearily and sank into silken cushions, closing her eyes with a sigh. Exhausted, she was yet well-satisfied with her evening's progress, having gone further than she had hoped. After some moments she opened her eyes to notice the presence of a tea tray. Rising with a bemused air to serve herself, she wondered who had brought it in so quietly as not to disturb her concentration. Agatha, she made no doubt, that paragon of maids who watched over her like a mother hen. A plate of wafer-thin cucumber sandwiches rested alongside the teapot and she helped herself to three.

Kate was the sole occupant of a library which had once belonged to her uncle, Lord Wellington, and which she had appropriated after his death some number of years ago. It was, therefore, masculine in character, but her own personality had eventually eclipsed this. Although it was not a large room, sofas, chairs, and tables of comfortable form were scattered about after a fashion. Hundreds of books lined breakfront bookcases designed by Robert Adam. While unable actually to design the house for Lord Wellington, Adam had lent a gracious hand to its final design and his touch was everywhere evident.

A light scratch at the door surprised Kate from her revery, and at her acknowledgment, the door was opened. It was Lady Wellington, a stylishly dressed woman in her early fifties often (gratefully) mistaken for her younger.

"Kate," she whispered timidly. "I do hope I'm not interrupting, but I simply must talk to you. I've been trying these past hours but you've been so intent, I hadn't the heart to be a distraction. But really, my dear, it's nigh onto midnight and I would like to retire." Gliding over the thick Aubusson that graced the room, she came to settle by her niece, smoothing her voluminous skirt as she sat.

"Of course you would," smiled Kate. "Indeed, I hadn't noticed the time and should hie myself to bed as well. Come have some tea, if you've a heart for it cold, it's been sitting that long." She proffered a cup to her aunt who waved it away with a face, being finicky in her preferences.

"How does the book proceed?" inquired Lady Wellington. "Is it nearly readied for a critique? Lord Saye is most anxious about its being completed in time for a spring printing. This very morning I had a short letter from him which I've brought for you to see. Do answer him yourself." She gave over the letter. "A word from you would be far more comforting than one from me. He worries so, but dares not tell you. Indeed—" She

6

frowned. "I do believe he is afraid of you and wonder I've never realized that before." She glanced suspiciously at her beloved niece. "Has he ever been given cause?"

Kate gave out a short laugh and shot her aunt a small mischievous look. "Well, I cannot marry every man who asks me, can I, dear aunt? He took the news badly, I fear, but will recuperate, I make no doubt." Kate grinned at her aunt's evident surprise.

"Well, this certainly is news to me," her ladyship exclaimed indignantly, toying with the rings on her fingers. "I had no idea the land lay that way, for I'm sure no one confided in me!" She was obviously more put off at Kate's secrecy than at the nature of the revelation.

"Please don't be angry," Kate implored, realizing that her aunt was sincerely miffed. "He asked for my hand last season and I tactfully declined. That's all there is to tell. It seemed so unimportant at the time, that I simply forgot about it. I had developed no tendre for him, you see."

"When John Daminel, fourth Baron of Scottish Saye, and head of the largest printing house in Europe, proposes marriage, it is not considered unimportant in some circles," her aunt quietly admonished. "Only in yours," she added depressingly. "But I'm glad you had such an elevated proposal, and naturally, since you do not love him, there was no other alternative than to refuse. I'll have no marriage of convenience in this house, I vow." She looked pointedly at her niece.

Kate colored faintly at this tacit compliment and Eustace Wellington congratulated herself on the girl's sense of humility. The chit was a great beauty, there was no doubt, and it never ceased to amaze her ladyship how little value Kate placed on this fact. The girl was twenty-four years and glorious. She had the finest eyes Eustace had ever seen and her ladyship had had many seasons with which to compare: they were blazing emeralds set in a face whose translucent skin compared with Dresden porcelain. Perhaps her lips were overfull, her ladyship considered critically, but she dismissed such imperfection as an actual asset preferable to those of London's thin-lipped debutantes (whom she held to be proportionately thin-skinned). Lustrous honey-colored hair, just now brushed severely away from Kate's face, was her niece's crowning glory. Eustace abhorred the style but agreed that it was probably more convenient when writing for long periods of time, as Kate was accustomed to do.

That Kate wrote, and wrote well, was another source of pride to the young woman's aunt, and Lady Wellington made no bones about it. The girl had a brain, as Eustace was wont to say, for better employment than on frippery and flummery. Of course when Kate had refused to travel down to London the previous season, there had been that dreadful row between them, but that was only because her ladyship feared an antisocial streak would develop in Kate. But Kate had wished to devote more time to her work, and had won out, and in doing so had established no slight independence. Eustace had taken it philosophically and could only hope for the best, next year.

As to Kate's yet unmarried state, Eustace had no qualms. The girl's parents had been killed in a boating accident off Italy when Kate was two, and Eustace had taken her in without hesitation, being childless herself. Neither had ever regretted it. Kate had been an affectionate child, and had given her so much pleasure, that the only thing Eustace feared was the day Kate would inevitably marry—on this account she had no doubts. But Eustace abhorred youthful marriages (claiming they led to "youthful indiscretions") and was secretly proud that Kate was still unattached, having been given time to mature and develop interests, to grow into a levelheaded young woman. Eustace had refused countless offers of marriage for Kate, confident that the right man would one day appear. This confidence made it easy for her to dismiss Lord Saye's proposal with a shrug.

All this flashed through her mind while Kate chatted on about the progress of her book. Actually, it had been written for the greater part by Kate's father, and saved over the last two decades as part of his estate. It was an historical treatise on the subject of Greek influence on Roman theater. Kate had stumbled on it a year ago, and after showing it to some of her father's colleagues, had been encouraged to complete it. She had been working on it for some time when it came to the attention of John Daminel, who was so impressed that he contracted for a private printing. Feeling her obligation, Kate was working hard toward its end, which accounted for the present timorousness of her aunt who had only lately come to terms with Kate's overlong, albeit temporary, withdrawal from society.

"Kate," she interrupted at length, knowing how one-tracked her niece could be, "did you notice the bit of frost we had this evening?"

"Yes, of course," replied the girl, casting a sidelong glance toward a window.

Her aunt read her shrewdly. "You mean, of course you did not. You haven't noticed anything these last few months. Not that there has been much to notice, for I have tried to keep things quiet that you might work more easily."

"For which I truly thank you," Kate stated emphatically. "I've noticed that much, I promise, and appreciate your very thoughtfulness. It must be very boring for you, what with no visitors and me with my nose in the proverbial inkwell. Your patience is a blessing," and she leaned forward to squeeze her aunt's hand affectionately.

"Think nothing of it, my dear," replied Eustace coolly. "I like being in my own home between seasons. London is exhausting and I can repair here at Randomm better than anywhere else. I never was a Bath miss. Besides, old houses like mine must be kept up in any number of ways and this takes time and thought. I am proud of Randomm and wish my late husband Carelton's standards to be kept. I hope I have been successful in my endeavor."

"Successful and more, Aunt," applauded Kate. "Indeed you are one of the best businesswomen in England, but you don't need me to tell you that," and she smiled to see her aunt blush.

Relaxing in the warmth of the fire, they were quiet for some time, then Eustace roused herself to talk of matters at hand. "I almost forgot what I came to talk about. Christmas is but four weeks away and I wish to invite a few guests for the holiday. I thought you might welcome the diversion, but if you have any objections . . ."—she hesitated—"naturally, I'll drop the matter."

"Oh, no, don't do that," Kate hastened to assure her. "I know how you would welcome the company. Besides I'm sure I will have privacy enough to continue my work."

"Well, I was hoping you would join in the festivities to some extent. You do need a rest," Lady Wellington noted with severity, "and Christmas seemed the logical time to impose one on you, and if I don't, I know not who will."

"You're quite right, of course, and I will help as much as you need," Kate agreed with some misgiving.

"Don't try to gammon me, Kate Barrister," her ladyship sniffed. "I don't seek your help but only some assurance that you will enjoy the holiday. You're thin as a pecked scarecrow and looking worn to the bone. People will begin to accuse me of being a taskmaster and never believe the truth of the matter. Oh, the questions they asked me when I went down to London without you!" Kate sighed to hear Lady Wellington launch into her favorite subject, having heard her lamentations before, but Eustace caught herself up. "Well, it's true, but I won't say any more on that head. But you do look awful," she could not help adding.

"In any case . . ." Kate prodded in her most quelling tone.

"Yes, well, in any case," Eustace took the hint, "there's no point inviting people if you are only going to spend all your time avoiding them."

"Oh, I won't spend *all* my time doing that," teased the girl irrepressibly.

"Kate," cried her aunt, "if you are going to be difficult . . ." but she was interrupted by a short hug from her niece.

"I'm sorry. Go on, I won't make any more jokes. Do tell, what have you there in your pocket?"

"Well, if it's all right then." Eustace considered slowly, ignoring the twinkle she saw lingering in Kate's eyes. "It's a list of guests I thought you might wish to approve."

"Oh, no, I trust your judgment completely and there is no one I'd wish to add. Constanza Markham is in Scotland visiting with her brother until April, and Emily Castorham has gone to Italy with her mama and also doesn't return until spring."

"Well, you know Madame Markham would never do in any case," huffed Lady Wellington. "Such a one I don't hope to entertain too often. The last time she was here she put the maids in a tizzy with all her radical mumbo jumbo. Some sort of nonsense about shorter hours." Kate laughed, only to receive a speedy reprimand. "Do you beware you also do not gain the reputation of a bluestocking, Kate! Society would close quite a few doors on you were this to happen, and I don't know how many I could reopen, even given my own unimpeachable connections. I fear just that, when your father's book is printed."

"Pah!" Kate disdained, "you contradict yourself. How could my father's book create a bluestocking of me? Besides, you forget the printing is to be private—only a select few will even know of the book's existence. I dare swear you never even mentioned it when you traveled down to London last spring."

"Nonetheless, one can't be too careful," Lady Wellington cautioned. "Jealous wicked tongues tell wicked lies."

"And so I promise to remember. Now whom did you think to ask?" Kate attempted to recall her aunt to the subject under real consideration.

"Oh, yes, well I thought to invite some half dozen guests, mostly old acquaintances. One of them is Cornelia Brougham though, who might show up with her son, if invited. Since her husband died, she's been so lonely."

"Don't give it another thought, Aunt. Lord Edward's presence will not disturb me in the least, and I have no fear of his pressing his suit again. He was put off in no uncertain terms, so if he makes his presence known, it will be under that condition."

"It shall be as you say, for I would dearly love to see Cornelia, if you don't think it selfish of me."

"I don't."

"Then there is Lady Sylvania Charles whom I 'owe' on account of having stayed with her during an extended weekend last May."

"You never mentioned it."

"I don't mention everything. But I must now because her daughter might accompany her. Pretty as a picture is Marguerite Charles, but otherwise an unknown quantity. She might perhaps serve to entertain Lord Edward, should he chance to show up."

"And James Charles?"

"In India. Can't stand English climate. But it serves to everyone's purpose, Lady Charles being unable to stand Lord Charles."

"This sounds dismal!"

"No, no, I've a few others in mind. It will work out, you'll see," she said hurriedly. "Well then, if the matter is settled, I shall take myself off to bed and bid you do the same. It's long past midnight and Agatha is sure to ask me if I've seen you. Your maid acts more a dragon every day, I must say. How do you stand her tyranny, my dear?"

Kate smiled up at her departing relative. "She means well, I dare say. We have our moments, of course. Do tell her I'll be up shortly." But Eustace shook her head as she closed the door, for Kate was already immersed in her work.

Two

Four weeks later, Lady Wellington's holiday guests began to fill the house. The first to arrive was Reginald Hallesley, third Duke of Landonshire. A handsome widower of middling age, he had made the acquaintance of Eustace some years ago. He admired her good humor and tenacity, and she, his cynical but honest wit. The two had become fast friends and corresponded, hence the invitation.

Eustace was coincidentally coming down the hall when the Duke was admitted by her butler. Her face was aglow as she gave him her hand. "I'm truly glad to welcome you to Randomm Manor. I wasn't quite sure if you would really come, but hoped for it all the while."

"My dear lady," he replied in mock severity, "it was a pleasure to accept your gracious invitation. To be perfectly honest, though, it was a welcome reprieve from my daughter Eloise's invitation. You see, she has just given birth to her third child, which fact boded ill for a peaceful holiday." But she heard the inflection of humor in his voice.

Indeed, Eustace was altogether pleased by his lordship's presence. She smiled to see him check the lines of his cravat in the hall's great beveled mirror as he handed his great coat to the butler. "I'm glad my home can be of service to you, in any case, my lord."

"But you must know I want to be here," the Duke smiled. "I understand that this is one of the last houses in England where the family actually decorates the tree, instead of delegating the chore to the servants."

"Surely you exaggerate," demurred Lady Wellington. "It's true we do decorate, but I'm sure I know of a dozen or more who do so also."

"Well, I've never done so myself and have come expressly to learn how."

"I thought you came to escape your grandchildren," she teased, "coward that you are."

"I'm a multipurposed man, Lady Wellington," and his eyes flickered, "but never, never a coward!"

Unsure how to respond, Eustace turned away, relieved to see a footman making his way toward them. "Crenolin will show you to your room, my lord." She made the Duke a deep curtsy, causing him to raise a brow.

"Quite formal today, aren't we, your ladyship?" he murmured, then turned to follow the footman disappearing abovestairs, while Eustace was left to sort out her confusion.

The Duke was shown to the master bedroom, unused since Lord Wellington's death. Dismissing the servant, he glanced lightly about the room to perceive the oversized green brocade bed. Fruit-wood tables flanked its head to display Etruscan-style lamps so difficult to come by. No doubt they were part of the spoils enjoyed by the late Lord Wellington during the Eygptian campaign against Bonaparte. His eyes came to rest on a central door, one obviously connecting to the mistress's room. Crossing to the portal he twisted the gilt knob to find it barely turned; he pushed—the door would not budge. "*Mais naturellement*—" he smiled slight-ly, and permitting a mental shrug, went about the business of making himself comfortable.

That evening, Eustace was late in coming down to the drawing room where family and guests were to reunite for dinner. Hence, the Duke and Kate were quite on their own when they became acquainted for the first time. Kate had dressed in brown bombazine more suited to a dowager and which did her little justice; but the Duke was a connoisseur of women and well able to see past Kate's unconscious pose. Discreetly, he took in the exquisite refinement of her face, her stunning green eyes, and ample (but well-draped) figure. He found his curiosity aroused while she, for her part, was almost egregious as she took in the Duke's meticulously adorned person. He watched with hooded eyes as she scanned his figure, his clothes and coiffure, and even his diamonds. He gave her points for being so brazen. He was even charmed to see Kate (having no idea as to his power or prestige) dismiss him as a dandy, his middling age apparently notwithstanding. This only served to point up (to him) her ignorance of good taste and deft appearance, but at least the chit was not easily bribed.

He wondered if a strong offence might not be interesting. "Miss Barrister, I've heard a little about you from your aunt. 'Twas inspiring, I do assure you. May I say how remarkable it is to find, these days, such noble pretension coupled with an (albeit) unassuming character. Although I am not one ordinarily accustomed to credit such sweet docility," he added quietly, thoughtfully, "as is suggested of you, by your aunt."

Kate looked up sharply at his curious words, ready to deflate such excessiveness. But suddenly she recognized the very glimmer of a twinkle about his eyes, although the rest of him was decidedly somber. She was certain she had been meant to, just as she was suddenly sure that she would not have, had he chosen not to allow it. It brought her up sharply; she felt she was undergoing a sort of test, and that he was forcing, nay—recommending, that she not betray too hasty an opinion of his person. Taking the hint that came from his eyes rather than his words, and following instinct rather than sense, Kate capitulated. She smiled, and he returned it warmly. Then the moment was over and their friendship established.

"Lady Wellington, you have hidden a briar rose," the Duke turned to greet her ladyship, who had made a hurried entrance at that juncture.

"I?" her ladyship murmured and mistook his

meaning. "I dare swear that is what all of London is saying, but you know it's not true. That I have hidden Kate, I mean. She's her own mistress and does what she likes. A briar rose?" she perked up. "I like that, I do. Thorns aplenty to prove the case—and, and prickly, too. But a rose, nonetheless, my Kate."

"Do tell," grinned her niece as she sipped Madeira and looked from one to the other. Perhaps a fortnight of company was not such a bad idea after all, she considered, and she settled back to enjoy herself in a way that she had not in many a month.

Within three days the rest of the party arrived, the sight of which almost caused Kate to revise her opinion. Lady Charles and her pale, willowy daughter Marguerite arrived amid a flurry of bandboxes and trunks, causing Kate to wonder if they were staying the winter. Lord Edward Brougham and his formidable mother, the widowed Countess Brougham, arrived half a day later. As one of the great London hostesses and a lifelong friend of Lady Wellington, she had taken a large hand in presenting Kate to the ton years before. The girl had been a moderate success, which made it difficult for the Countess to comprehend Kate's marriageless state. She had no idea that her beloved son listed among Kate's rejected suitors: she would never have understood that, either. Although most of the guests knew each other by sight, Lord Edward was able to greet the Duke with some effusiveness, being a close friend of the Duke's son and a member of the Corinthian set of which said son was also a member. Edward could hardly be blamed for not realizing this last to be scant recommendation to his lordship, who frowned upon the set for its frivolity.

The following days before Christmas were spent quietly at Randomm. The weather was crisp and clear thus allowing Kate, Marguerite, and Edward to take long walks in the snow while their elders kept to the manor playing whist, reading or conversing, or participating in any number of other divertissements.

Two days before Christmas, Kate reluctantly lent her manuscript to the Duke as she had promised some days previous. He promptly took himself off to the library while everyone else elected it a perfect day for a drive in the Wellington sleigh. The ladies had purchases to make, as well as a desire to sight-see, and Edward agreed to escort them.

Marguerite Charles was a vision as she came down the steps to the waiting sleigh attired completely in white fur, her golden ringlets confined by a matching hood, causing her to seem paler than usual. Kate was dressed in a sturdy gray wool dress shortened for practical purposes and thus revealing even sturdier half boots of Spanish leather. Her face half hidden by a cloak, Kate smiled at the contrast she made with Marguerite while Lady Charles, always ready to exploit an advantage, discreetly arranged that her daughter be seated next to Lord Edward. Well, that certainly made things easier for Edward, Kate mused, as the party set out at a leisurely trot.

The fact was, Edward had been in a quandary ever since he arrived at Randomm. He had cared for Kate for quite some time, but her repeated rejections of his offer of marriage were beginning to embarrass him. A gentle, but somewhat self-engrossed man who sported muttonchop whiskers and a small belly, he had not yet thought to lay down his claim tactfully. He had come to Randomm intending to make one final, romantical proposal, on Christmas Eve naturally, and look elsewhere for a wife if Kate rejected him. As Marguerite Charles gazed soulfully into his eyes, he was confirmed in the sensibility of this plan.

The day went splendidly. The drive was uneventful and an amusing hour was spent exploring the local monastic ruins, evidence of one of Henry VIII's more exuberant quarrels with the Italian church of the 1530s. The party then wended its way down into the village where another hour was spent gazing into its few store window-fronts and making numerous purchases, including gifts for the servants at Randomm. Finally, the party stopped at a local inn renowned for its pastry and China tea. They had been settled not more than half an hour when John Longer, their coachman, was ushered into the parlor.

"Begging your pardon, your ladyship, but I knew you'd want to know . . ." John began slowly.

"Know what, John?" sighed Eustace, who knew that every word must be dragged from him.

"The sleigh split a runner."

"A runner! Impossible. You must be mistaken."

"No, ma'am. I'm not mistaken. Begging your pardon."

"No, I know you're not mistaken," she said exasperated. "I was only being . . . never mind, my good man. How came you to notice this?"

"Inspecting," he illuminated.

"Well, we'll have to find another sleigh in which to return."

"There ain't any. I asked."

"Well then, you must have Jake Turner repair it immediately. It will be dark in less than an hour, and the Duke will wonder at our delay."

"Jake can't fix it nearer than thirty minutes. Got a flash cove in a hurry."

"John, you must appeal to the man's gallantry and explain the situation," Sylvania Charles condescended to opine.

"Wait," interrupted Kate, "I'll go myself and speak to the man. Perhaps I'll have more success."

"I'll accompany you," offered Edward, but it was obvious that he did not relish going out into the cold again.

"No, you stay," smiled Kate, putting a hand on his arm, "you haven't finished your tea. Besides, Jake Turner is an old acquaintance of mine and this is a good opportunity for a visit." So saying, she hurriedly cloaked herself and hastened to the forge before anyone could stop her, her hair ribands threatening to come unbound as she ran.

As she arrived at Jake Turner's shop, she spotted the splintered runner leaning against the wall. Dismissing John to a nearby taproom, while admonishing him to have only one pint, she entered the forge to see Jake hammering away and quietly approached his workbench. He looked up to see her, a broad smile lighting his face.

"Miss Kate," smiled the elderly wainwright, "how have ye been? It's been that long I havna' seen ye. Although me missus says you were up to the house, Tuesday last, I think."

"I'm fine, Jake, and I see that you are also. And I hear that business is also good this evening." Kate smiled gently at the old man who used to shoe her childhood ponies and now cared for her dappled mare.

"Business is good, I will agree. But if you've come to set me to work on yer runner, I canna', that's a fact, and so I told yer John Longer. I'm being well paid, 'tis true, for this piece o' fancy work, but it seems the gentleman's in a might o' hurry, so . . ."

"But Jake, surely a stranger could not take precedence . . ." Kate began, only to be startled by a deep voice from behind.

"I do hope you are not going to exploit your friendship with Mr. Turner, ma'am, for I should take it in very bad form if you did." Kate spun around to see a large figure shrouded by the shadows of the shop.

"I did not mean it in quite that way, sir," stammered Kate, embarrassed to be caught out. "It's only that I have three elderly ladies in my charge and do not like to have them kept waiting," she explained.

"Ah, yes, you're with the party I saw entering the inn. By now they must be comfortably ensconced in front of a blazing fire. That is not terribly inconvenient, I think. Far better than being here, don't you agree?"

"Perhaps that is so," she agreed, peering unsuccessfully into the darkness. "But if Jake cannot mend the wheel immediately, it means they must return home in twilight. I cannot agree that that is convenient, sir."

"They have less than an hour's wait," returned the man, unmoved. "That is not too awful. I'm sorry to seem so lacking in gallantry, but I'm in a great rush myself. You may deliver my apologies to your mistresses," said the man with finality, and turned and walked out into the yard. If she had not been so angry, Kate would have found it amusing to have been taken for a servant.

Kate bade a terse good night to Jake and followed the stranger outdoors. The man was more visible as they met, and as she looked him over, his cold eyes stared back in turn, secretly admiring the honey-colored hair that threatened to tumble free of its riband. But his face was unrelenting, and she knew it, as he stood silently to watch her pass. She glanced at the split runner, then up at the twilight sky, and gave a noncommittal shrug.

"It would seem that chivalry is dead in England," Kate could not resist saying as she moved toward the gate. An arm shot up to block her passage and her heart quickened in fear.

"Alas, 'tis true," the stranger agreed. "Edmund Burke would sorrowfully concur: to be succeeded by 'sophisters, economists, and calculators.' But you're a plucky young one, I can see that you will easily survive on your own."

"No thanks to you, good sir," Kate returned scornfully.

"Goodness, you must be one of the sophists!" smiled the stranger. "Has your mistress been too lenient with you? No doubt you lead her a merry turn and perhaps she would thank me for curbing your tongue. Indeed, methinks I will," and before she could stop him, he had caught her up in his arms, entwining her hair in his bold fingers. "I'm one of the calculators, you see," he grinned, and was suddenly kissing her hard. For a moment Kate was startled, but her wits returned and she began to push him away. He released her quickly, a sardonic look in his deeply-lined face. Lines of dissipation, Kate divined, not incorrectly.

"Now you may really despise me, but, I must admit, the pleasure was all mine." She raised her hand to slap him and he caught it mid-air, his dark eyes reflecting amused indifference.

"Surely you've been kissed before? Behind some pantry, I'll warrant. Those green eyes could entice the devil himself, and I seem to have proved no exception. Now, take my kiss as a compliment and do be a good girl and run off." He gently turned her about, and giving her a slight push forward, disappeared back into Jake Turner's forge.

Kate spun around to stare furiously after him,

rage mounting within her breast. Hateful thoughts ran through her head as she returned to the inn, where she met Lord Edward in the anteroom, donning his cape.

"Kate," he exclaimed, "I was just coming to find you. Where have you been all this time? We were beginning to grow worried."

"Oh, I heard a kitten meowing in the alley and returned it to its mama."

"Really, Kate . . ."

"Oh, not now, Edward, I'm very cold and would beg a cup of tea." Walking past Edward she entered the private parlor, presenting only a picture of a slightly flushed young woman. She walked directly to the fire and made a great show of warming herself, all the while fending off questions about her disappearance.

"John was right. The gentleman is in a great hurry and refuses to allow Jake to work on our wheel. But since it is only a matter of minutes before he is finished . . ."

"But how long will he be?" interrupted Lady Charles, concerned about returning home in darkness, although Eustace and Cornelia only continued to drink their tea.

"Yes," echoed Marguerite, "how long will Jake Turner take to finish, for I fear to meet a highwayman."

"Never think it, my dear," Kate said smoothly, "there hasn't been a highwayman near Randomm in over four years. And besides," she added, happy to further a good cause, "Edward is well able to protect us from any mishap." Turning red at this unexpected attention, Edward mumbled something about his abilities.

"All this is very well," pursued Lady Charles, "but exactly how long will it take for Jake to set us on the road?"

"We should be returning within the hour," Kate assured them. "I have seen the runner and the damage is very slight."

Everyone grumbled a bit but finally agreed that matters could be worse. Cornelia Brougham ordered a fresh pot of tea and the group settled down to wait. Kate was able to secure a quiet seat and mull over her encounter with the detestable stranger: a more arrogant man she would never hope to meet. To remember how he had treated what he took for a servant girl was positively infuriating. It was appalling to think how the quality often treated the lower class. Then she remembered his kiss, his hard cold passion, and yet—the inexplicable warmth of his lips. Her thoughts ran on in this vein until she mentally reproved herself and made a halfhearted attempt to join the general conversation. A boy came by at five o'clock to say their carriage was ready and it was a cheerful group that bade good evening to the beaming innkeeper and his wife.

Three

Lost a grip on yourself, thought the swiftly galloping horseman. A pair of green eyes glance your way and you fall to pieces. But such eyes, he sighed, as he remembered kissing the girl with an abandon he had not felt since childhood. His blood swam at the memory and he laughed at himself for being such a nodcock.

Soon he was passing through iron gates, all such thoughts disappearing as he concentrated on his surroundings. He made his way up a narrow road which led to a house well-situated on the side of a hill. On closer inspection, he found it to resemble a *"cottage ornée"* rather than the manor he had been led to expect. Its intimacy charmed him and he wisely reserved judgment of its interior, knowing its apparent simplicity could be illusory. He took the main steps in two and a stern-faced butler opened the massive doors within moments of his knock.

"I'm told the Duke of Landonshire stays here as a house guest," and as he took the answer for granted, strolled into the house. "My horse awaits stabling, if you would be so kind."

The butler frowned, but at the same time recognized the quality of the cape he was handed in such an offhand manner. "His lordship is here, sir. May I ask who is calling?" he inquired in his most depressing voice.

"His son, my good man, his son," laughed the man. "Now you may please announce my arrival, for I would have words with him," and he flung a guinea into the air, then handed it to the butler.

"This way, sir," said the startled butler, showing him into the drawing room.

The young man observed the good taste which had taken a hand in the decorating. Everything was muted and conveyed great serenity and he willingly sank himself into the nearest sofa. He was gazing at what was surely an original Titian when his astonished father entered.

"By Jove, this is rich. Whatever are you doing here, Alex? I thought you were on your way to Cumberland for the holiday. Have you lost your way?" inquired the Duke with a very straight face.

"Well, Father, that is not the warmest greeting I've ever encountered! Are you not pleased to see me?" The younger man frowned as he stood mud-splattered before his father, his disheveled black hair falling close to wary gray eyes.

His father looked him up and down and laughed. "I'm always pleased to see you, Alex. But you must concede this an unexpected place to come upon you." He glanced again at his son's muddied attire. "Nothing of great import has happened?" asked the Duke, suddenly alert.

"No, father, I beg you do not be alarmed at my appearance. I was merely feeling a reprobate for not spending Christmas with my family and sped down to Sherringhouse. When I had arrived, Eloise informed me of your whereabouts, and I must say I was surprised. But I was enlightened by the sounds of her new squalling babe and decided to likewise take a hint. The place is in an uproar and I simply don't understand why Eloise doesn't hire a better housekeeper. But there, I made my excuses, lamely I admit, yet Eloise understood."

"The thought of listening to that infernal racket for three weeks was more than I could bear," grumbled his father as he glanced ruefully at his son. "I'm glad you quite understand."

"Yes, well," grinned his son, "in any case, I'm on my way back to London and thought I would stop and bid you join me. It's dashed lonely in town this time of year, what with everyone scurrying home for the holidays."

The Duke's brow rose. "My dear boy, I shouldn't like to disappoint you in your apparent hour of need, but I'm sure I have no wish to return to London. I'm having a delightfully peaceful Christmas here with some old friends and intend to stay on through the New Year." And as if to prove his words, he began to light a cigar, a thing unheard of in most homes, which emphasized his hostess's hospitality.

"Well, if that's the way you feel, Father . . ." But the man's words faded as a cacophony of voices filtered in from the adjoining hall. Suddenly Lady Wellington burst through the door, trailing behind her a beleaguered footman whose arms overflowed with packages. Lady Charles followed, as did Lady Brougham.

"The others have gone to change for dinner and so should we . . ." Sylvania began loudly by way of greeting, but her voice died at the sight of the newcomer and Cornelia also sent the Duke a quizzical glance.

"Ladies," coughed the Duke delicately, "may I present an unexpected visitor, Lord Alexander Hallesley, Marquess of Landonshire. Also known as my son. Come to save me from the dismals of the holiday season, bless him. Always thinking of me."

"My father jests," smiled the Marquess charmingly. "I'm the prodigal son returned home for the holiday only to find my father no longer in residence. I tracked him down here and stopped to wish him merry. As I do you also," he added, but omitting to bow, quite done in after spending the day in the saddle and not about to do the civil.

Their ladyships, not amiss to the proprieties but only tremendously curious, gave the young man a thorough going-over. Taller than his father and of a greater stature, he was definitely not a figure to be ignored. He had a shock of black hair that fell about his face of strong but regular features. He had a great deal of presence and it seemed to the women that it culminated in his eyes, remarkable eyes of steel-gray that were at the same moment impudent, yet charming.

The Duke did the introductions and Eustace rang for sherry. "You stand in need of a hot meal or I'm much mistaken, young man."

"I must admit to only a light luncheon but will be in London in under two hours, if I leave promptly. I'm sure my cook can arrange something," Lord Alexander added quickly, not wishing to be shanghaied for a week with some elderly ladies and a sardonic father.

"Nonsense," Sylvania exclaimed in her abrupt way, and a matchmaking mama at heart. "You're obviously tired and must be very hungry. Lady Wellington has a spare room, I'm sure, and will not object to your staying the night."

"I wouldn't dream of putting her to any trouble."

"Alex, did you know," interjected the Duke, "that Lord Edward Brougham accompanied the Lady Brougham this trip?"

"No. No, I didn't. Is Edward here?"

"As I have said. And since he has talked of you in such glowing terms it would hardly be fair of you to leave without as much as by-your-leave to the poor fellow. He would be chagrined." The Duke smiled ironically as he met his son's eyes.

"I wouldn't think of it," murmured the young lord, and turned to his hostess with a faint sigh. "If I may take you up on your kind offer, my humble thanks."

"You needn't humble yourself," exclaimed Eustace. "After all, you were going to spend the holiday with your father and here he is. Besides which, my butler tells me there is snow in the air and it would not do for you to be caught in a storm. Why, I would never forgive myself. Dinner is in thirty minutes, so you will have plenty of time to change," she concluded inflexibly, but with sincere warmth.

Sensing that he was fairly caught, Lord Alexander accepted her invitation graciously, secretly promising himself to be off at dawn. A servant was called to fetch in his bags, and the Marquess shown to his room, as everyone scattered to theirs.

Some one hour later, Kate was giving herself a final glance when she heard a scratch at her door. Dressed in unrelieved gray wool trimmed with white dimity at the neck and cuff, she looked an exceptional study in severity. Agatha had brushed Kate's hair the requisite hundred strokes but the poor maid had not been allowed to dress it, but to only watch in misery as Kate bound it at the nape. As Marguerite Charles entered in a swirl of pink muslin, red rosebuds dotting her dress and golden hair, Kate knew she had done the right thing. She smiled at the picture of contrived innocence Marguerite affected and hoped Lord Edward would be charmed, having no doubt at the effort that had gone into the girl's dressing.

"Were you expecting company?" Marguerite could hardly desist. "Mama says we have some."

"No, I wasn't," Kate assured her as they walked down the stairs. "Who is it, do you know?"

"No, I don't." Marguerite pursed her lips. "Mama only stopped by my room for a moment, but I could tell it was someone important, for she bade me change my gown." She left off speaking as Cornelia joined them.

"Marguerite, we're looking excessively fine this evening," she drawled, instinctively knowing it was not for the benefit of her son. And staring pointedly at the older girl's gown: "And it's a rare day in May that I do see you dress, Kate. Where did you get that gown? It's the only color I've seen you in since . . . since I don't know when. Indeed, I begin to grow suspicious at the way you do dress down."

Kate demurred and hid her eyes for fear Cornelia would see the laughter there. Marguerite looked her over with renewed interest but dismissed the matter as inconsequential and hurried into the drawing room.

"Lady Eustace," she smiled, stooping to buss her hostess. "I do hope I haven't kept you waiting," she apologized quite charmingly.

"No, dear, you're just in time," Eustace assured her, "and looking as lovely as ever." But the young woman saw her ladyship's brows rise as Kate entered with Cornelia.

Marguerite, impatient for information, kept to her hostess's side. "I understand we have a new addition to our house party, ma'am."

"Do you doubt your mother's word?" Lady Charles huffed.

"No, mama, begging your pardon. I was just being polite," replied the girl, all pink and innocent. But before any argument could foment, the butler entered with two gentlemen following in his wake.

There was little doubt that the two were father and son. Both were unusually tall men, and in their well-fitted evening clothes, gave evidence of great vigor. Both were dressed in velvet, the father in brown, the son in black. And both sported frothy cravats of the finest lawn, and cuffs of the same material.

Lord Alexander went straight to Lady Wellington. "Ma'am, I can only thank you once again for your kind hospitality. One day, when you are in London, I hope to be allowed to repay you in some way." He bowed with a flourish which captivated her ladyship at once.

Kate gasped at the sound of his voice, and gave the speaker a sidelong glance from beneath her lashes. Identifying the gentleman instantly as the stranger at Jake Turner's forge, she struggled desperately to keep control of her rising rage as she watched everyone fawn over him hastening to be introduced.

"What a faradiddle, sir," Eustace was saying, "with such a large house it's the least I can do and in no way any inconvenience, as you may guess." Then, turning to her right: "You remember Lady Charles and Lady Brougham, whom you met when you arrived?" He did another leg, but not as deep as the first, in deference to his hostess, who appreciated his subtlety.

She gestured toward Marguerite, who was obviously aflutter at the entrance of such a Corinthian. "Marguerite Charles, only daughter to Lady Charles." Lord Alexander smiled at the girl, now comprehending her mother's earlier insistence that he stay the night.

"Charmed," he bowed, guessing that in her youthfulness, Marguerite would be in raptures over his small grace.

"And behind you," Eustace continued quickly, not wishing to allow Marguerite any limelight (having taken an instant dislike to the "simpering silly" as she was wont to privately call the poor girl), "behind you are Lord Edward Brougham and my niece, Miss Kate Barrister."

"Edward," cried Lord Alexander, cheered by the sight of a familiar face, "what a sight for sore eyes." They clasped hands enthusiastically.

"Alex! The way you do turn up positively boggles the imagination. How came you here? Looking for the old, er . . . ah . . . the Duke?" Lord Edward hastily amended.

Alexander laughed. "Yes, that's it precisely. But what brings you to these parts?" At which point Edward gestured to the figure seated to his right who had escaped the Marquess's greeting. Lord Alexander made motion to exchange courtesies to the gray little figure and bowed over a proffered hand. But when he glanced to Kate's green flashing eyes, he blanched with remembrance. "Ma'am" was all he could say, and said it twice, much to his own mortification.

"My lord," returned Kate tight-lipped, fingers trembling in his.

"Kate and I are old friends," Edward explained. "I could never forgo an invitation to Randomm, so interesting as she makes it."

"Interesting, Edward?" but Alexander Hallesley took the situation in at once, one brow raised high. Was it possible that Edward was truly interested in this bland woman who dressed so badly and who didn't seem to have one redeeming quality? But was it possible that this was also the same woman who had made his heart beat so merrily only hours ago?

"Yes, I daresay Miss Barrister can be full of surprises." His black eyes were unreadable and confused his friend, but Kate understood him very well. Only the timely entrance of the butler, who announced the serving of dinner, saved her from embarrassing both of them.

She was never sure how she got through that dinner, refusing all but a morsel of green goose and pear-in-aspic, which she forced herself to eat for fear of causing comment. But she watched miserably as Marguerite cruelly cast Edward Brougham aside to flirt outrageously with Alexander Hallesley, who responded within the strictest mode. Poor Edward turned to Kate for consolation, but she could barely return a syllable, while the Ladies Charles and Brougham chattered away like magpies. Lady Eustace and Sir Reginald Hallesley sat at the other end of the table, oblivious to all.

Four

The gentlemen were admonished not to linger over their port as the ladies rustled their way across the hall into the drawing room. The elder women arranged themselves by the fire, while Kate and Marguerite found themselves separate settees, the conversation immediately directed to the newcomer.

"What an exceptional young man the Marquess is," commenced Lady Charles eagerly. "Not precisely handsome, I think, but with a definite hint of *'je ne sais quoi'* about him. And so tall, taller than his father. My word, I can't remember the last time I met a man of such height."

"An excellent conversationalist," contributed Lady Brougham noncommittally, having no wish to pursue any aspect of Lord Alexander which might lead to comparison with her son, who would inevitably fare at a disadvantage. Not so old that she might be unaware of the impact the Marquess could make on women, she had, besides, been on the ton too long not to have seen his charms proven times untold, from afar. In all fairness, she did like the young Marquess and was secretly pleased that her son ran in his circle. But she'd seen which way the wind blew (she thought) between Marguerite Charles and her beloved Edward, and such a rich young lady was to be cultivated, hopefully, with the least competition.

Eustace was embarrassed by Sylvania's blunt remarks and thankful for dear Cornelia's more temperate approach. But to her mortification, the "simpering silly" also spoke up, proving herself her mother's daughter.

"For my part, I think he's exceedingly handsome, and an heir to a dukedom, no less! What good fortune he stopped here," she added carelessly, unaware of the fulminous look sent her by Cornelia. Although Kate had no thought of entering into the conversation, she could not resist a swift glance in the girl's direction. She caught Marguerite stealing a glimpse in a mirror, and their eyes met briefly, but Marguerite only shrugged and turned away.

"I have heard," said Cornelia sternly, loyal to her son's interests, "that he never trifles with a woman for longer than a month, and that he never flirts with one younger than twenty-five, being impatient of their youthful contrivances."

"Tut, tut," snapped Lady Charles, "I have never yet met a man whose mind could not be persuaded to a cause, especially when the cause is a pretty girl. In any case, even if he is the type to occasion a light flirtation, well, it really wouldn't matter.

It's an opportunity to help arm my girl against the cajolations of London society."

Cajolations? It was all Kate could do to contain a sudden rise of merriment. She caught her aunt's sympathetic eye, and between the two, they almost went off into the whoops. Only the greatest sense of decorum allowed these ladies to practice containment. Ultimately, Kate was sobered by the thought that the women were talking about a "gentleman"; the application of such a term, she secretly knew, could be used only in the loosest sense toward Lord Alexander.

Thankfully, there was no continuing the conversation for the men had been quick over their port as promised, and were joining them at long last. Indeed, they had only lingered so as not to insult the wine steward, who took notorious pride in his lady's cellar. Lady Cornelia was right in thinking that her son would not bear up well in comparison with the Marquess of Landonshire. Although Lord Edward was not unhandsome, his stature was short and he tended toward corpulence. The Marquess, on the other hand, was tall and lean, his gray eyes discomfiting yet compelling. Kate sympathized with Cornelia's fears and wished she could enlighten that poor lady as to his dreadful true character.

The Duke settled himself in the vicinity of the fire, but immediately the young men entered Marguerite Charles demanded a rubber of whist which they couldn't possibly refuse. Kate was solicited to make a fourth and hoped her face was

43

carefully schooled, for inwardly she was in turmoil. She considered it good luck to partner with Edward, the irony of which did not escape her, for he was infamously bad at bidding. Yet it enabled her to converse minimally, thus concealing her confusion, although she could not (unfortunately) close her ears to the conversation. The cards were dealt and she studied them as if she'd never seen a deck in her life.

"I say, Alex," Edward began as the game got under way, "I've come across the greatest pair of goers, everyone says so. Got 'em at Tattersall's and could show you so tomorrow."

"Well," smiled the Marquess, all congeniality, "we might take a ride and see what you're about tomorrow. I've seen your bargains before though, and won't go easy on you if you've been had."

"You won't be disappointed, my lord. In fact, you'll probably want to buy 'em." Edward grinned and proceeded to overbid on his trump. "They're not for sale, by the way."

"Good," smiled Lord Alexander, "then I am spared the possible embarrassment of having to refuse that which I didn't want in the first place."

"Embarrassment?" hooted Edward, " 'lor, I never knew you for one to mince words!"

"No, I suppose I do take what I want when I see it, when I can get it—if it's available."

"What's that supposed to mean?"

"Oh," smiled Lord Alexander, "just a commentary." Was not Kate just a shade more pink? He couldn't be sure; she had refused to look his way all night.

Marguerite, all rosebud ecstasy, fluttered her blond lashes artfully as she had practiced many times before her mirror: "Lord Alexander, are you a member of the Four-in-Hand Club, for I hear that you are a noted Corinthian?"

"Of course he is, my dear," Edward answered for his friend. "One of its earliest members, silly goose." He blithely ignored her indignant look. She tried a new tack.

"Do you play much at cards, my lord?" She smiled sweetly, although she probably knew everything public there was to know about the Marquess of Landonshire, being an avid devotee of the *London Gazette*'s societal columns. "I'm only a novice myself," she added lightly.

"I have been known to score a point or so," he smiled, "but you have nothing to fear, I shall lead you to no excesses." He was amused to finally see Kate forget herself so much as to roll her eyes heavenward then return intently to her cards.

"La, sir," Marguerite carried on, "I think you are teasing for anyone can see you are a true gentleman." Lord Alexander discreetly took note that Kate's face was now under complete control.

"Well, in any case," pouted Marguerite prettily, "it's all very well that you men are to go riding tomorrow, but what shall I do for amusement?" Sensing her indiscretion, she quickly explained, "Kate is so busy in the library all morning I

45

cannot look to her for amusement. She works on that manuscript every day."

"Manuscript?" Lord Alexander echoed, greatly surprised.

"She's the closest thing I know to a 'bluestocking,'" Marguerite informed him mischievously, but to her dismay, Kate laughed.

"Would that I were, my dear child," smiled Kate gently, speaking for the first time. "But I suspect I've a long way to go before I'm worthy of that title." She laughed at Marguerite's obvious shock and Lord Alexander's raised brow.

"An unusual aspiration in the main, don't you think?" he suggested.

"Unusual because it is rare," Kate rebuked him, "not because it's impossible. Women are simply not educated to standards reflecting their capabilities—their true capabilities I mean."

"I dare say," responded his lordship, perturbed. "Yet I have not met many women so dissatisfied. Or at least they have not said so."

"Perhaps it is that you have met only a limited variety of women, Marquess. Or perhaps you never asked," snapped Kate, flashing green eyes huge with implication.

"I dare say," murmured Lord Alexander Hallesley, attending her words, but deciding not to press the issue—for the time being, at any rate. A bluestocking was a novelty and would bear closer watching. Especially such a looker, he grinned to himself, and returned his concentration to the cards.

At length tea was served and the card party broke up. Kate took her cup to a damask sofa set slightly apart from the main group, hoping to be forgotten, but within moments she was staring down at two feet planted firmly by her side. She had no need to look up to identify their owner.

"May I join you?" asked the Marquess, in his rough familiar voice.

"I have no choice, sir, do I?" she murmured, chagrined that he should seek her out.

"Not if you want to avoid a scene, my girl." Startled by his tone, she looked up to see a scowl on Lord Alexander Hallesley's face.

"Smile," he commanded. "It will look better," and as he seated himself all trace of his own anger vanished.

"I've come to apologize," he announced bluntly, annoyed at finding himself in this position. Kate said nothing, eyes expressionless.

"I think you know the matter to which I refer," Lord Alexander continued curtly.

"Hush, I beg you sir. Do not put me to the blush by making this a public matter."

"My apologies," he lowered his voice, "I only meant to say that what happened this afternoon was . . ." his search for words failed. "For my part, I meant no real harm," he finished lamely. Damme, she wasn't going to make things easy, he realized, in exasperation.

"Consider the matter closed, my lord. I have already put it out of my mind," Kate promised unconvincingly, head bent to avoid his eyes.

"I don't believe you for a moment, so please don't expect me to thank you for your graciousness. I want to apologize for my behavior and implore you to forgive me. I can see you have a hard heart, but really, I refuse to leave until we make amends." As he spoke Lord Alexander Hallesley knew that nothing could possibly sound less contrite, even to this drab of a girl.

"You're a guest in my aunt's house, Marquess," Kate returned stiffly, "and for that reason alone I am willing to forget the matter. But you may as well know that I consider your behavior to be the mark of a dissolute character."

Lord Alexander was astonished and greatly indignant, so used was he to being pampered by the opposite sex. "I will not allow one small stupid accident to define my character so abysmally. Surely you've been in similar awkward straights? You might consider that all I actually did was to kiss you, the attraction being undeniable. An unchaperoned woman is prey to all sorts of advances, of which mine was the mildest form. I promise I am not often so susceptible, and in fact, have never been so before! I regret causing you any distress."

Infuriated to hear such a high-handed attitude, it was all Kate could do not to box his ears. "No, sir, I have never been in 'similar, awkward straights' as you put it, nor is it my habit to prey on less able people," she retorted. "Besides which, what happened was no accident, although I will agree it was small and stupid for your part. And," she added sharply, "I don't believe you really regret my distress. Or that you even credit it," she stared up at him defiantly.

"My word," he stared back amazedly, at the same time startled by the brilliance of Kate's eyes. "You certainly have your opinions! Well, you're quite right, I don't credit your distress. Damned near most provoking thing that's occurred to me in years, and not exactly under conditions one would attribute to a lady of quality, much less any lady of genteel circumstances!"

"And who are you to talk of provocation, sir, or even of quality?"

"You baited me, my dear."

"Lud! You exerted physical restraint on my person when all I did was deign to criticize your lack of gallantry. An unwarranted and excessive retaliation, don't you think?"

"Well, I did warn you I was a calculator."

"You, sir, are a boor, that's what you are!"

"And you, ma'am, are a brown-nosed snob. Whatever was I thinking to have lost my head over such a one as you?" Lord Alexander Hallesley shot back furiously. "I can see that you're in no mood to be forgiving, but then, most women are the stubbornest things walking. But there, I really should not abuse you so, your being that helpless and all." He smiled coldly.

"Lord, how you do go on," Kate smiled her most insulting smile, and was pleased to see the handsome Marquess turn red.

"Madam, you must excuse me before I cause a

scandal and wring your bloody neck," and with that last he rose abruptly and walked away to join the others.

Suddenly confused, Kate made her way to the warmth of the fire and lost herself among the flames. What demon had made her speak so when the poor man was making his apologies? she wondered remorsefully. She had not meant to be so inflexible, and felt uncomfortable with her behavior. And yet, his was the most insincere apology she had ever heard. Or was it only that he was unused to humbling himself and did not know the way of it? Her head spun with a myriad of thoughts that would surely follow her to bed that night and allow her little sleep, she suspected.

Five

Kate woke late next morning to the purposeful bustling of Agatha, clearly heard from the adjacent dressing room. Smiling at her maid's notoriously unsubtle manner, Kate stretched and yawned and turned drowsily to glance out the window. To her surprise there was evidence of new fallen snow, and jumping out of bed to take its measure, Kate was horrified to see they had been overspread by no less than a blizzard. Lord almighty, whatever would she do stuck indoors all day with Edward Brougham and Marguerite Charles? Lord ... oh goodness! She remembered Lord Alexander Hallesley! That abomination from London, how to deal with him? And it was Christmas Eve, she reminded herself and sent a wistful glance toward her bed. It was tempting to feign a headache, or perhaps a cold—a few sneezes would do—and crawl back under the nice warm sheets. . . .

Agatha quietly entered and espied Kate standing by the window. "Ah, you're up," she grumbled, "and in good time, too. I've a list for you as long as my arm, and her ladyship has asked to see you directly after your breakfast. Oh, and Lord Edward Brougham wondered if you'be be down soon, and that was at nine-thirty, yes, and cook wants your advice on the plum pudding, and . . ."

"Enough," cried Kate laughingly, giving her bed a last long look as she shrugged herself into some warm, practical woolens. Able to descend within twenty minutes, the first person she met was Lord Edward who was just leaving the breakfast parlor.

"Kate, my dear, a very good morning," he hailed her heartily.

"And a good morning to you, Lord Edward," she returned cheerfully as she passed hurriedly into the parlor eyeing the sideboard hungrily, having been unable to partake of last night's dinner.

"Kate, dear Kate, I simply must talk to you," he trailed assiduously behind.

"Yes, Edward?" Kate returned absent-mindedly, piling her plate high.

"It's about us, you know," he put forth awkwardly, pulling nervously at his ear.

"Edward," Kate advised in her most quelling manner, "I have not yet had my coffee. You don't realize, but should be warned: I have no manners until I've had two cups!" She almost laughed aloud to watch him take her meaning and tactfully back off.

"But of course." He blushingly reconsidered and made a note to catch up with her later; which was just as well because at that very moment Lord Alexander Hallesley entered the room.

An unusually tall man, his whole frame took the entire height of the doorway as he paused to observe the occupants. Giving Kate a curt nod, and Edward a small smile, he proceeded to seat himself at no small distance from his hostess. The Marquess had spent some time the night before thinking about Kate although coming to no conclusions. He deeply regretted his behavior at Jake Turner's, but only inasmuch as it reflected on his status. It was not that he took his peerage so seriously, or demanded concessions from others, but he hated to feel vulnerable and Kate's criticism cut him to the quick, having always prided himself on acting socially circumspect. Which he had (until their unfortunate meeting), confining his baser impulses to the demimonde. Of course the silly chit would never believe that, her being so damned "countrified." It was all so awkward he had even thought to pack up and leave that morning. But one look past his window had dashed his hopes, and so he had descended without alternative. Not that he needed one, he could readily see, for the minx hardly glanced his way.

Actually, Kate could hardly spare him a glance, so busy was she cultivating an air of insouciance, having been quite unnerved by his sudden entrance. His physical presence made an unexpected impact on her but she attributed her palpitations to a natural antipathy for the man. She was grateful for Edward's presence, and even the saving grace of Marguerite Charles's arrival, and recognized the humorous aspect of this.

"Oh, la," Marguerite posed delicately at the parlor door for effect. Dressed in a morning gown of pale blue muslin, a matching riband running through her golden curls, she was indeed a charismatic picture.

"I'm so very late, aren't I? But Mama says a woman must needs her rest," she giggled and waited for a response. Kate was aghast at such self-centered simplicity and it was all she could do not to laugh out loud. She caught the Marquess eyeing her curiously and turned self-consciously away.

"Really, my dear," Edward gently took up the threads of conversation, "do let me serve you some coffee."

"Coffee, ugh," grimaced Marguerite. "I never, never drink that poison. It gives one blotches and dark circles, my mama says. I'll have tea, thanks," and she watched him pour. "But where are the servants?"

"It's Christmas Eve, don't you know," Edward explained. "The house is in an uproar, begging your pardon, Kate." He smiled Kate's way apologetically.

"Never think it, Edward," Kate serenely returned. "It's always so on Christmas, and only natural for everyone to be in a taking, what with one thing or another. But everyone enjoys it, much as they complain; it's traditional, you might say."

"Mama would never countenance such goings

on," Marguerite informed the others with great aplomb.

"Well," smiled Kate sweetly, although friends who knew her would look beyond this particular smile, "your mama would never live in the country either, would she? Tell me, why did you accept our invitation, if you really so dislike such pastoral surroundings?" She saw Edward groan inwardly and, amused by his stern look, sent him one back as Marguerite guilelessly continued.

"Well, Mama said it would be better than ..." but the poor girl, suddenly aware of being caught out, put a hand to her mouth.

"Quite right," interceded Edward gracefully, and at the same time directing Kate a speaking glance. She averted her eyes, her lips trembling with laughter. He deftly turned to the Marquess. "Alex, don't you want anything? I'm used to seeing you wolf down a hearty breakfast."

"Just so," smiled the Marquess, "I was lost in thought but you make me attend. Just so. Shall I serve myself?" he casually addressed the air, wondering how far Kate's manners would carry. Although still very angry with her, the last few minutes had shown him that she was not to be entirely without a sense of the ridiculous—except perhaps where he was concerned, which fact made him even more angry. He was suddenly overcome with a desire to punish her for teasing him so; oh yes, that could quite possibly be a source of amusement.

"I suppose I shall have to serve myself," he

sighed sententiously, although a stint in the Hussars during Napolean's defeat had made him more than self-sufficient.

"A marquess serve his own breakfast?" Marguerite cried, horrified.

"God forbid," Kate muttered and rose to do his bidding.

"I beg your pardon?" smiled Lord Alexander.

Kate didn't bother to answer but only set before him a veritable mountain of food: cold ham and beef cooked to a turn, double-yoked eggs, buttered toast and an assortment of marmalades, the entire coffee urn, creamer and sugar bowl.

"Anything else, your lordship?" Kate inquired coldly.

"Not for now, thank you. Later perhaps," he returned quietly, appreciating the flash of her eyes.

"Then since you are content, I have things to do. *Bon appetit!*" Kate curtsied and made her escape. Really, she sighed, she must remember to have Agatha send a breakfast tray to her room in future or she'd never eat in peace!

Kate went in search of her aunt and found her ladyship arbitrating (none too successfully) a quarrel between cook and housekeeper over the recipe for currant bread. After settling the dispute and dismissing the servants, Kate and Lady Wellington spent a half-hour conference dividing the household chores to be overseen. They then went their separate ways so that soon everything was running smoothly. The problems had been double-fold, for as the family prepared for the holiday evening so did the servants set up their own festivities, replete with dinner, guests, and gifts. Around three o'clock, Kate found she had completed her tasks, and knowing she could no longer avoid her guests, forced herself to put in an appearance. But mysteriously, no one could be found, so she cheerfully took herself off to her library to spend an hour over her own work. She had just settled down when rustling from a high-backed Queen Anne chair drew her attention. Peering into the corner, Kate was startled to see the Marquess rubbing the sleep from his eyes. In that moment he charmed her, but she steeled herself as he began to speak.

"Penny," he murmured, his eyes flickering. "Oh, it's you. I thought it was . . ."

"No, it's me," Kate interrupted coldly. "And who is 'Penny' if I may be so bold? No, I'm sorry, don't answer that question. I'm afraid to hear what you'd say."

"Penny," Lord Alexander straightened himself, "and you are ever so bold, is my valet, an indispensable chap, and intelligent in the bargain. What are you doing here?" he demanded, making no attempt at manners. "Why aren't you doing your social graces?"

"Everyone has disappeared: catnapping like you, I make no doubt. I thought to . . . but what are you doing here? This is my private library, don't you know?" Kate snapped.

"Is it now? No, I didn't know. Ah, yes, I remember, you're the budding authoress—the bluestocking," he returned sarcastically, vaguely wanting to hurt, and succeeding, he made no doubt, as he watched his words take their measure in Kate's stricken eyes. So, again he had touched a tender spot.

Kate made no response, but only passed a hand quickly over her brows. "I ever seem to rate so poorly in your eyes, I wonder at its source. I'm not so strong as to best you in sport, and I've never been up to Oxford, so perhaps you may tell me what the threat is for you."

"Threat? You overestimate yourself, my dear. My animosity, if one can call it that, springs from a natural antipathy to long-winded females." Lord Alexander settled himself more comfortably with a purposeful air. It was his wish to intimidate this country miss, but Kate was not easily fooled, and only winced at his apparent want of tact.

"Long-winded, my lord? I've never been called thus; you are obviously not used to . . . never mind. I expect you're referring, in your extraordinary way, to my refusal of your apology."

"Ah, yes, that! Well, I admit it did pique me; but don't give it another thought," he shrugged carelessly.

"As you say, I don't. But perhaps you do?" Kate was curious to see how honest he could be, for she was sure he was more than "piqued."

He stared deeply, aware that she was provoking another confrontation. The implications of his answer were certainly pregnant, as he had no doubt she was conscious, and he wondered where she was heading, and why.

"Well, as to that," he murmured, deciding to take her up, "I suppose it comes down to a question of honor. I acted a bounder—trespassed, you're quite right—over class boundaries, as it were. Took advantage. I do see how you might see it, and you were quite right to take me to task." He suddenly rose and taking a deep breath, turned to smile at Kate quite charmingly. "But so few do, it took me by surprise; there, now you have the situation."

Kate was flustered by the Marquess's abrupt reversal and by this intimation of his charm. Unsure how to respond she floundered, then decided to chance his veracity, or at least, his persuasion. "Very well, I do. I did regret my vehemence, but I was very angry, you understand, and you were exceedingly provoking."

"So I was, my dear, as you were exceedingly enticing, it comes down to that." He wasn't seeing the dowdy the others saw daily and accepted without question. Indeed, she was to him the young beauty whose pretty hair had come undone with the loss of a velvet riband, a riband which, strangely enough, he yet held in his possession. He took in her eyes, her oval face and full lips and was surprised to feel his heart jump. "As I've already said, I am not usually so susceptible."

Kate reddened. "You try to discomfit me, sir, and appeal to my sense of vanity. But I have none—sense, I mean," and caught herself wryly. "Sense of vanity, I mean."

"Surely you jest," Lord Alexander stated flatly, clearly disbelieving.

"No, really," Kate smiled at him for the very first time. "It's all of a piece to me, what I look like or even how others do. You, I suppose, are used to having women fall all over themselves for you, and not even think twice about it. I live a different life, and do object vehemently to such insubstantialities." Her eyes flitted over his person lightly. "In twenty years you may be portly and bald. What will you offer a woman then, my lord?"

"My fortune," he returned calmly.

"Will that satisfy you?" she asked curiously. "If you say yes, I suppose I must believe you, but it would not suffice for me, and sounds a most depressing future."

"Well, you certainly make it seem so. But I never think of the future, it comes so fast upon itself." But he was thinking very hard nonetheless, and was annoyed that she made him do so. "Why have we never met in London, do you think?" the Marquess crossed over to neutral territory.

"We travel different circles," Kate laughed. "Mine would bore you no end, I promise you."

"You don't know that for a fact. Will you be in town next spring?"

"Yes, for the season. But mostly for the printing of my book—or Papa's, I should say. Lord Saye has offered to print it and I am grateful, it goes without saying."

"Papa's?" Lord Alexander asked, not understanding, and listened as Kate explained.

"My word, you really are a bluestocking!"

Kate laughed, hugely amused. "Really, I'm not. There was so much there, it was just a matter of sorting it all out. Papa's notes were too valuable to be allowed to gather any more dust. It was the least I could do, and I've strong loyalties, you see. Plus a phobia against being bored."

"Bored? How could that be? A woman has little excuse for that!"

"London bored me," Kate returned seriously. "It was never enough for me only to attend assemblies and routs, or musicales which were mostly second-rate. Flirting bored me," she added pontifically, "and anyway, I was never very good at it."

Lord Alexander laughed. "That's a first for me, and hard to credit. But I'll take your word," and he threw up his hands good-naturedly.

Kate had no doubt she really was hard for him to comprehend. He probably never met a woman in his life who had refused to flirt with him.

"Well, shall we make our peace, Miss Barrister? Your terms are harsh, but it is more than I deserve, and besides, I like your style."

"Terms?" Kate's brow rose questioningly.

"Well, you're an unusually forthright woman, you see."

She eyed him distrustfully, then capitulated. He offered her nothing, this she based on his past behavior, and he had carefully made no promises.

But he had caught her fancy, so few men did, that she only sighed and smiled. "You're right, I am an odd commodity."

"And you'll give me a run for my money," he said deadly serious, and left her to ponder his meaning as he made off to change for dinner.

Six

Kate was right. The household had seemed to sleep away the afternoon, but by eight that evening all were assembled in Lady Wellington's elegant drawing room to celebrate the eve of Christmas. The ladies were dressed most festively in satins and lace while the men complemented them in their fashionable velvets. Garlands and mistletoe embellished the room and a huge crystal bowl of Lady Wellington's special punch had been wheeled in to greet the holiday in style. It was apparent to Kate, even yet descending the stairs, that the merrymaking was already under way.

"Holla, Kate! Come see what we're about," Lord Edward called as she entered the drawing room. Tinsel, ribands, bibelots saved over the years, incense, candles, gooseberry vines, and all sort of accouterments lay strewn around a magnificent evergreen which had been cut by the gardener earlier that day. The Ladies Charles and Brougham, along with Lord Edward and Marguerite, were busily sorting them and decorating the tree; Lord

Alexander lounged by the fire; the Duke of Landonshire had designated himself to serve the punch while Lady Wellington confided the secrets of its content, a prized family recipe.

"Do come help, Kate," pleaded Marguerite in a rare burst of fellowship. "We're simply overwhelmed and need every hand we can muster, Lord Alexander's notwithstanding." She sent the Marquess a petulant look but his eyes betrayed no interest.

"What's this, Alex?" asked his father, handing him a glass of punch, "no holiday spirit, man? Drink this down and we'll change that. I know of at least three hands which thoughtfully spiked this bowl, no names mentioned, naturally. It's guaranteed to equal anything served in London-town."

"Thank you, sir. I make no doubt of its strength, if you are serving it up. To be sure, Lady Wellington, my father plays a subtle hand," at which her ladyship gently blushed.

"Kate," the Duke drew his arm through hers and proffered the devil's brew, "quiet, also? Eustace, I swear these young folk have truly lost the art of living. Get ye under the mistletoe, girl, and give these young pups something to think about! Yon Alex has a lean and hungry look. Blushing, Kate? Bless me, it runs in the family," and he laughed at his own jollity.

"Father, our friends are unused to such badinage and know not what to make of you."

"My son, I've had that same problem many

times these last fifty years," but he left off to complete his rounds. "Lady Charles ... Lady Brougham ..."

In good time the tree was trimmed, gifts assembled beneath, and Lady Wellington's staff called to receive theirs, with their patron's good wishes. A sumptuous dinner was then laid, after which the servants were dismissed for the night to enjoy their own sociality. It was a peaceful group that later resettled itself in the drawing room, dull with good food and wine.

"Play a minuet," Lady Brougham begged of Kate. "It's been that long I haven't heard one and I don't care a jot if I date myself."

"Of course," smiled Kate, making her way to the pianoforte, glad to be of use, for the holiday spirit had somehow eluded her.

"A dance," clapped Marguerite, glancing in the direction of the Marquess. "Now if I only had a partner," but her hopes were dashed as Lord Edward made his way toward her.

"Charmed," he smiled and she had no choice but to join him in a pirouette while the Marquess volunteered to turn the pages for Kate. Marguerite watched jealously as they shared some small exchange, sensing that a change had taken place between them. Biting her lip in consternation, she proceeded to flirt with the amiable Edward; there was no point in sulking, Mama had often counseled—it only caused wrinkles. And there was always tomorrow, she promised herself.

"They dance well," Alexander commented quietly as he turned the score for his hostess.

"Yes, they do." Kate glanced the couple's way to see Marguerite giggle at some tidbit of Edward's. "She's a very graceful creature and should be a great success when she's formally presented next year."

"Yes, she's graceful," Alexander agreed, "except when she talks. Then I wish I were miles away. How she does go on, and so nonsensically—but then, there seems to be little in the way of discouragement."

"She'll find her milieu, I make no doubt. I'm sure it's just nerves. She's young, you know."

"You talk like an old woman," Alexander smiled skeptically. "Have you never had a case of nerves?"

"None that I can recall, my lord," Kate returned a shade too complacently.

"I shouldn't wonder," Alexander murmured, but Kate caught the twinkle in his eyes and smiled shyly, remembering their truce.

The impromptu musicale lasted until well past midnight, when Kate laughingly called it quits. She was rewarded, as were all, with Christmas grog and the fire was built up one last time. They all clustered round and caroled until the last embers fell and Eustace took note of the time. Everyone fell on each other with fond goodnights, made fonder by dint of their toddies. As the guests mounted the stairs, Kate discreetly made for the library for a habitual last minute check on her papers. Flopping down onto a sofa, glad finally to

66

be alone, she found that her peace was to be short-lived.

"Kate, may I have a moment?" Edward suddenly peeped round the door, entered and firmly closed it behind him.

"Oh, Edward, I was just going up for the night. Can't it wait until morning?" she pleaded, "I have the most excruciating headache."

"Of course, my dear, so sorry." But ignoring his own words, he came to sit across from her. "Is there anything I can do?"

"Nothing, thank you. My maid will mix a tisane when I retire." Agatha would have thought that very droll, for Kate was a notoriously bad patient, always resisting medicaments.

But Edward had intended to be fobbed off no longer. "My dearest Kate, we're finally alone. Won't you let me speak? No, you have been putting me off this week and longer, but I am determined you shall hear me out." He took a deep breath, then: "I love you, Kate. I want to marry you."

Kate's eyes flew open. "Edward, please, we've already discussed this matter. I can't accept your offer. I don't love you."

"So you've said," returned Edward thoughtfully, "and I've given that much consideration."

"Really, you oughtn't have," Kate deprecated with a sigh.

"Oh, but I wished to, and have come to a conclusion, besides. I'm willing to marry you, notwithstanding your feelings, and am confident that, given enough time, you will come to return my affections. Assuming you are not already engaged?" He cast her a worried look.

"Do not think it. But wherefore should I wish to 'come to' as you say? Why do you ask so little for yourself?" Kate demanded curiously.

"Kate, to be very blunt, it has come to my attention you need caring for, and that I can provide easily. Secondly, I don't understand why you think I want so little when I would value you above all else."

"Edward," Kate responded haughtily, "I do not need caring for! Although perhaps *you* would be the better for the love of a wife, it is not going to be me. Suffice it to say, the deep affection which I do have for you would not, is not, enough to draw me into the bonds of holy matrimony! Not with all it entails, thank you very much." She rose to give him her back as she stood by the fireplace.

"I can offer you everything," Lord Edward persisted bravely in the face of her firm stance. "Think of the wonderful life we could have, you and I together. We could go far, become a ton couple. You would be feted wherever you went. Surely you must be bored here in the country, and London holding so many attractions."

Kate turned to smile at Edward's naive assessment of her character. "You are wrong there, you know. London holds no interest for me. Indeed, whatever would your friends make of a brown-nose like me?" she laughed. "If my mouth didn't get me into trouble, why then, my lack of elegance would certainly deter my social success. I'm a homing pigeon, my dear good friend. The ton would simply not know what to do with me. I remember quite clearly the last season I was there: all arms and legs—the gawkiest thing you ever did see. And absolutely incapable of conversation ... anyway, the kind expected. No, Edward, it would not do," she concluded with finality.

"Really, Kate, you underestimate your charms. The season to which you refer was eons ago. You were a child, now you are a woman. With the right clothes, a good hairdresser ..."

"Edward, your persistence is become vexatious. Above all else, I don't love you and would never marry without my affections being engaged."

"Kate, what I feel ..."

"Edward, you prevaricate. How can you want to spin such a Banbury tale? I saw how susceptible you were to Marguerite Charles' lures only this very evening!"

"Miss Charles only plays with me to make Alex jealous, as we are all very aware. No, 'tis you I love, I swear it," he insisted and was suddenly beside her, catching her in his arms. Quickly kissing her squarely on the mouth, he just as quickly released her. "Forgive me, Kate, but you are so maddening."

"Edward! How could you?" she admonished sternly, stifling a giggle at the ludicrous situation she found herself in. "I cannot, cannot, marry you and that's my final word!" She stamped her foot in annoyance. Raising her arm dramatically to point to the door, she was amused by her performance, and that Edward could elicit such high drama from her.

Mortified, Lord Edward shuffled in its direction, knowing his business to be at an end. "Kate, I do adore you," he flung out mournfully, "but I promised myself this would be my last attempt to bend you to my side. I won't bother you again. But of course we may be friends, although it will take me time to recover from my . . . my wounds." He missed her fleeting smile, which told that she knew he was play-acting, to a degree.

"Thank you, Edward," Kate returned softly, "you are very kind and I am grateful we yet remain on friendly terms. But I am confident you don't love me and that one day you will know this and be grateful I did not accept your offer." As the door closed quietly, Kate stood staring after him momentarily lost in thought, a smile hovering about her lips.

"Charming, simply charming," came a voice from another direction. Kate whirled around to face the Marquess half-hidden in the shadows of the French doors.

"How dare you, sir, how dare you?" she spluttered indignantly.

Lord Alexander slowly approached the fire. "How dare you, ma'am, is more the question," he sneered.

"Whatever do you mean? Skulking behind curtains, minding other people's business!"

"That's doing it a bit brown, don't you think? I

was merely taking a stroll enjoying a cigar, and couldn't avoid witnessing such a charming scene."

"You, sir, were spying," Kate charged contemptuously.

"And you, madame, were flirting," Alexander returned derisively, "first with me, then with Edward. And not for the first time, no doubt. And such an innocent country miss you played me today. What a gull you must have thought me to be taken in so easily by a lot of high-sounding notions. Words, just words."

"I am not a flirt," Kate snapped, "you have misconstrued everything! Isn't it just like you to jump to conclusions, asking questions when it's too late and you have done your damage."

"All right," he said tightly, "I shall strive to cultivate a little restraint and listen to your explanation. Speak woman, that I may be enlightened." Alexander seated himself with an air.

"I owe you nothing," Kate hissed, "much less any explanation of my behavior, but I do not like to see you so complacent. The fact of the matter is that the whole thing was unexpected. I was in here tidying up when Lord Edward barged his way in, without my permission, mind! That's all there is to tell."

"But that's not all, is it? I saw much more, I'm afraid. And I distinctly saw you smile as he left. Can you explain such amusement?" his lordship drawled, but his face was taut and Kate sensed his disbelief.

71

Frustrated, she began to shuffle papers around her desk. "I was smiling at his persistence, if it need be known. He has proposed before but refuses to take no for an answer. He's very childish in some ways. Stubbornlike, if you want. And was enacting such a Cheltenham tragedy," she sighed.

"Very neat, my dear. I wish you may admonish me like that. A more desirable nanny I could not imagine."

Kate's lips trembled at the insult Lord Alexander carelessly flung out. It was apparent he was in no mood to be convinced. "Get out," she fumed, beginning to feel rather misused by fate. But in a thrice, the Marquess had reached her side and spun her roughly around, his fingers digging painfully into her shoulders.

"I won't leave until I've had my say. And tears won't hinder me," he added, in case she was the sort. "I kissed you yesterday, prompted by the same impulse which just prompted Edward; you're a dashed good-looking wench. I end up acting in a morality play, abasing myself before your purportedly monastic soul, while that pup simply gets sent to bed without supper! Where's the logic of it all? I find your behavior erratic and fickle and will not be made a fool of."

Kate pried at his fingers. "I was not making a fool of you, nor doing any of those things you say. There's a world of difference between you and Edward. Oh, don't you understand anything?" she cried impatiently.

"You're trying to talk your way out of this, but

it won't fadge. And if you want to be kissed, you should have a man do it, not a boy like Edward. There is a world of difference," he mimicked, but suddenly, to his surprise as much as to hers, she was in his arms and he was kissing her. Kate froze against the swiftness of his attack, her thoughts and feelings ajumble, then suddenly she was unable to resist. She responded to him deeply—and he felt it, and she knew that he did.

Then Alexander released her roughly, almost flinging her aside, and Kate found herself grasping the desk for support. Her hand flew to her burning cheeks as she peered up into his face. She could see he had paled but that was all she could fathom; their eyes locked for some moments. Then, without uttering a single word, Alexander walked out of the library.

The Marquess departed for London at dawn, leaving behind vaguely explanatory missives for his hostess and his father. He left no note for Kate, nor did he believe she would expect one.

Seven

1817

Spring came early to London that year of 1817, and Hyde Park sparkled with a daily fresh rain that brought the early foliage. In April, Eustace and her niece also arrived for the season, Eustace heaving a sigh of relief when they entered the gates of the city. That good lady had never been easy that Kate would not back down at some moment and refuse to accompany her. Her niece had been inordinately withdrawn most of the winter, burying herself in her work, so that Lady Wellington was unable to broach her and ascertain her feelings. But during the last week of March, Kate had quietly packed her trunks and announced herself ready to depart whenever Eustace desired. Eustace had been dumbfounded, but wisely withheld comment except to privately bid her maid also pack in order that she could set them on the road to London before her niece could change her mind.

John Daminel was ready to publish Kate's father's manuscript, quietly of course, for it was written to appeal only to certain scholars of that time. Therefore, once arrived in town, Kate spent time at the printer's going over the galleys with a thoroughness that was the despair of the poor man. On those days she would return home with ink-stained hands and her aunt would call for lemon water and glycerine, while at the same time admonishing her niecè for not having kept her gloves on. The rest of Kate's time was spent renewing old acquaintances—especially Miss Emily Castorham's, and going to a few select routs and assemblies; only once did she tool her carriage around Hyde Park. Her relative sobriety created an ambience of sophistication which appealed greatly to the haute ton's dowagers, but Kate put the younger members of society off, although it must be said, 'twas unwitting, for her part. She simply had no style, much less any visible humor, and her assets were not well advertised; hence, people stood in awe of her, although no one quite called her a spinster. Needless to say, Eustace was not pleased by Kate's lack of enthusiasm, and was at a loss how to remedy the situation, as she confided to Emily Castorham one afternoon, who listened sweetly but made no suggestions.

On the other hand, Lady Wellington was not impervious to a slight change in her niece, which had begun she knew not when. Yet, if she found Kate gazing abstractedly into empty air, she assumed her niece was worrying over the success of her book. If she had to ask Kate a question twice before it was heard, she assumed she was fatigued and would cancel a rout or two. In general, Eustace was only slightly concerned, although she kept a guarded watch.

Kate Barrister was neither of these things, but in truth suffered from a malaise which puzzled her nearly as much as her aunt. Slowly she was beginning to come to a few realizations—primarily, she was beginning to find all a bore. Ton parties suddenly seemed to have a sameness about them, and a few excursions to Almack's confirmed to her its latent insipidness. On rides to Hyde Park friends would chatter away and only she knew how mechanical were her responses.

One day, after her umpteenth trip to the printer's shop, Kate returned home and delivered a tirade regarding the poor man's turtle pace, a tirade which surprised her aunt as much as it did her. It was on this occasion that, being gently remonstrated by Eustace, Kate burst into tears, a thing previously unheard of and which caused her good aunt to immediately send for Doctor Cambers. He diagnosed exhaustion and sent the girl to bed with a double dose of laudanum, which only served to give the girl a spanking headache next day. Of course, she seemed calmer after that, which fact lent support to Eustace's admiration for the good doctor.

Kate never suspected her distemper to be in any way connected to her brief encounter with the Marquess of Landonshire, for in fact, she had put him completely out of her mind months past. Initially, she had been shocked by his behavior, but her own in comparison, caused her no small discomfort. The memory of her capitulation in his arms (that disastrous night in the library) made her burn with shame and had probably disgusted him no end, she was sure. She remembered the look he had sent her, the way he'd abruptly left the room, his silent departure at dawn. She had been lowered by it weeks after, and in the end Lord Alexander's part in the drama became minuscule, while her momentary lapse assumed gargantuan proportions. Kate convinced herself that all blame for their ghastly behavior lay at her door: after months of unaccustomed strain at her writing table (composing, rewriting, and editing) her sensibilities had been brought to unusual pitch. Hence, at the time of her association with the Marquess of Landonshire, she had been in a weakened emotional state and liable to any sort of outburst. Thus had he found her easy prey to his advances, as did Lord Edward Brougham, she roundly reminded herself, giving greater merit to this argument. Although acknowledging that she had not responded to Edward with the same degree of intensity, she had yet dismissed this as irrelevant to the main issue. She finally made herself promise that, in future, she would guard against such a letdown of her defense, and that the strictest self-discipline would insure this. The Christmas "unpleasantness" would serve as a reminder of her potential weaknesses, and with this in mind, Kate sought to ease her stricken conscience. Convinced that she would never meet Lord Alexander Hallesley again because they

78

traveled different circles, the matter rested and was forgotten. Until the fateful night Kate dragged poor Emily Castorham to a private salon held by her good friend Madame Markham, the famous feminine socialist.

"Oh, Kate," Emily wailed from the depth of their carriage where she huddled for warmth, a comely girl with brown curls and quiet brown eyes. "Why did I ever let you talk me into this? I'm not the type for these affairs." She pulled her cashmere cloak more closely around to ward off any dreaded chill. She sent Kate a stricken look which took in that woman's drab garb, causing her to wince. "I'd much rather we were going to Celestine's party. Do you think you could change your mind?"

Kate smiled, but said nothing and only peered out into the evening rain. Somber weather for a somber night, she considered, taking wry note of the water squishing about in her half-boots.

"It's not too late to change plans," she heard Emily plead and turned to give her friend her full attention.

"Look, you promised to come," she reminded the girl, "so don't talk such fustian, Emily. I won't leave you and you won't have to say a word but only sit and listen to the others. You are an intelligent girl and only want a bit of learning to polish you off," Kate teased. "Really, there's more to life than assemblies and balls!"

"Oh, pooh, Kate, it's you who talk fustian. Never going out anymore except to these . . . these meetings! And your clothes! And hair! My goodness, Kate, I do love you so, but people are beginning to talk." Emily saw Kate's lips tighten and quickly leaned forward to squeeze her hand. "I'm sorry. Have it your own way, but I do wish you'd confide in me sometime." She was astonished to see Kate's eyes fill with tears.

"Emily, dearest Emily, you are a patient little woman and I'm utterly thankful for it. But there's nothing to tell so let's have done. Anyway, we're here," and brushing aside her friend's concern, Kate leaped down from the carriage. She dismissed her coachman, opting to hire a hackney for their return, as the salon would often run late.

Constanza Markham held salons only four or five times a month, and very different they were from the main. An issue of only the most serious import was selected as the evening theme: female equality, British conscription, colonial expansionism, political expediency, child labor, or some such like. Certain guests were elected to debate the subject, and when the dialectic was over, an elaborate tea was served, during which everyone else was encouraged to air their own views. No liquors were served, nor were cards played; there was no dancing, and it goes without saying, no music was provided; ostentatious dress was discouraged, flirting was inappropriate. All was terribly conservative, with an eye toward elevating in the most unpretentious manner.

Emily was exhausted when, four hours later,

Kate blessedly motioned for them to leave. It was eleven o'clock.

"Did you enjoy yourself?" Kate enquired of her friend as they watched Madame Markham's footman hail them a hackney.

Emily yawned delicately, then purposefully brightened. "Oh my, yes, I'm numb with shattering thoughts," she smiled as they clambered into the hackney and set off for what promised to be a jabbing ride. They had not gone very far when the carriage lurched forward throwing them onto the floor. They heard the horses kick and the driver curse, then all was suddenly quiet.

"Mums," apologized the driver, who had opened the door abruptly, scaring them half to death. " 'Tis beggin' yer parduns I is, but we's jest lodged inter a rut. 'Tis anuther team I'll be needin' to kerry us out, but yer ladyships 'ull hafter gee on alone."

"Oh, no," cried Emily, "it cannot be." Kate jumped from the carriage to see. "It's true," Emily heard her call, and collected their belongings with a philosophical sigh.

"There's an inn not far," the driver advised and held out his hand to feel drops. "Rain's comin'. Better ye be makin' haste, ye can get another cabman there. Sorry. 'Twere no fault o'mine," he complained and disappeared round the other side of the vehicle. It was very dark and totally silent but for the clinks of the driver unharnessing the team.

"Oh, well," shivered Kate stoically, "nothing

like a midnight stroll in London, in the rain." She smiled weakly.

"If Mama finds out," Emily observed, "I'll never hear the end of this. Unchaperoned, no less." She wrung her hands, causing Kate to laugh quite loudly, albeit nervously.

"Emily, have you no spirit?" Kate wiped the rain from her face, then tucked her friend's arm in hers, and set them about at a no-nonsense, brisk pace. As they rounded the corner, Emily let out a screech as a massive coach tore down the street in their direction. They flung themselves against a wall as the coach dashed by, splashing them with mud. Some yards up, it ground to a halt and a man jumped out and made his way towards them.

"Ladies, are you all right?" began the gentleman, who left off with an astonished shout: "Kate Barrister, what in damnation . . . !"

"Oh, Edward," Kate cried, immensely relieved to hear a familiar voice, "you nearly killed us. And look at our clothes." But she laughed all the same as he began to fumble for his handkerchief, finally coming up with a hapless square of lace. "Never mind," she smiled and began to wipe herself with the corner of her cloak, while Emily followed suit.

"What are you doing here?" Lord Edward demanded, and Kate explained briefly. "But you must let me see you home," and they were grateful for his offer and allowed themselves to be steered, shivering, to his coach. When he put his head in the coach, they heard grumbles of protestation; then he helped them step up, so that fate might deal its deadly blow. There, to Kate's eternal horror, sat Marguerite Charles, and beside her the Marquess of Landonshire.

"Miss Barrister," cried Marguerite, red-faced at being caught in the untenable position of riding unchaperoned with two bachelors.

"Miss Charles," Kate responded coldly, but merely nodded to his lordship as they all settled in and the coach lurched forward. Kate hardily determined not to sink with mortification, but she would needs hold her chin very high against the barrage of questions which were to follow.

"Where have you been on such a dreadful night?" Edward began most forwardly.

"I was to Madame Markham's, if you must know," Kate answered stiffly, counseling herself not to squirm as she caught the Marquess taking in her muddied appearance. "And this is my good friend, Miss Castorham." She glared at Edward in rebuke for not having inquired. Emily merely smiled and sat quietly as introductions were made, glad to have been passed over as a little mouse.

"Madame Constanza Markham's?" Edward bluntly returned to the original subject. "That stone-faced harridan?"—and Emily was hard put to stiffle a giggle at such a forthright description.

"I beg your pardon?" Kate squinted dangerously, "I don't remember criticizing your friends." She was pleased to watch Lord Edward flinch in the lamplight as he caught her implication. A quick glance at the Marquess saw him raise a brow although he chose to remain silent.

"Miss Barrister," Marguerite spoke in a languid voice, an affectation she had acquired since her come-out some weeks before. "Do I take it correctly that you like that sort of thing? I've heard the most enervating stories about the goings-on at Madame Markham's and Mama says she's not at all the thing."

"She would not be, for such a refined creature as yourself," Kate said quietly, praying she might keep her temper in check.

"And did you enjoy yourself, Miss Castorham?" Marguerite purred, her condescension unconcealed.

"Oh, yes," smiled Emily sweetly, "so charming, so knowledgable—Madame Markham, I mean. I learned ever so much, you know, and am grateful to Kate for agreeing to take me."

"Forced you, I'll vow," snickered Edward, at which the Marquess smiled slightly, to Kate's consternation.

"Untrue," exclaimed Emily, sensing the tension and not about to let her friend down. "I take leave to differ with you, Lord Edward Broom—uh, pardon, Brougham," and she sent Kate a conspiratorial wink. Kate was astonished at her friend's outburst and touched at the support Emily was attempting to supply. "Constanza Markham is a brilliant woman and an evening spent at her home is . . . is enlightening! Far more valuable than any evening you seem to have spent." Emily was pleased to watch Edward's mouth fall open, pleased with her newfound power.

"Quite right, Miss Castorham," spoke up Lord Alexander for the first time, and she sent him a grateful smile. "We have not met, but I know your mother well. I live a few doors down from your house, you may remember."

"Oh, yes, my lord," she replied shyly, slightly awed by his address. "I am spending the night with Kate," she explained needlessly.

"Ah, yes, Miss Barrister. How do you fair? It's been an age since last we met," Alexander declared, his face betraying no emotion.

"I do well enough, your lordship," Kate muttered, caught unawares and unable to think of a better response. For his part, Alexander refused to respond to her tone.

"Do you attend these meetings often?" he continued coolly, his long white hands resting on an ebony cane. "I am curious to attend one, you see."

Kate could not tell if he was serious and doubted it very much. "Do you my lord? But I am afraid you would be bored. No gambling, no wine, and no women in your style."

"I'm not so dissipated as all that, my dear." His eyes flickered in annoyance. "And as for women, well, don't you worry over my style! I prefer to do my own picking"—he continued to cut—"about which matter you know nothing, I assure you."

Kate fought back tears, grateful they were nearing her home. But Marguerite was not finished, having taken pleasure in Kate's discomfort and deciding to press the advantage.

"Miss Castorham, Miss Barrister, are those uniforms you wear?" she asked in a demure voice. Kate reddened, perceiving Marguerite's intent; it was all she could do not to kick the wretch as she sat back so complacently, swathed in silver tissue.

"No, Miss Charles." Kate summoned the last of her dignity. "They are studies in expedience. You do understand the concept of expedience?" she gave the girl a long, hard look.

Marguerite fairly flew at Kate's words. "I heard that you had all but given up society. Is that what you mean by expedience, Miss Barrister? Are you announcing your spinsterhood?"

"Not really, Miss Charles," Kate retaliated, inwardly raging, "I would never be so unsubtle."

"Come to think of it, Kate," Edward pursued tactlessly, "I haven't seen you at a single ball this month! Not at Almack's, or anywhere! Have you really been hiding yourself?"

"Yes, dear Edward," she snapped, losing all control, "and taken up knitting, and go to bed at nine, and oh, all manner of wonderful things!"

"Oh no, not really. Not at nine," he protested quite foolishly. "On the other hand, I'm sure I've seen you about, Miss Castorham, and am glad to make your acquaintance, finally," he added with a generous smile, and Emily bowed her head to hide her perplexity.

But Marguerite was miffed at this paltry exchange and would not let go. "Then you're not a bluestocking also, Miss Castorham? Heavens be praised. I wondered . . ." She left off mischievously and Emily paled at her implication.

But just then the coach drew up to Lady Wellington's mansion and Kate, fairly flying from the confines of the coach, barely stopped to thank Lord Edward for his timely assistance, so rattled was she by the conversation. Being closest to the door, Alexander accompanied them to the steps of Kate's house.

"Miss Barrister," Emily distinctly heard him call. But to her horror, Kate all but slammed the door on his hand and most certainly in his face. Then she took the stairs in two, making a dash for her room while Emily followed softly behind.

Kate cried for close to fifteen minutes as Emily held her close. Then, bleary-eyed, Kate lifted her tear-stained face to pose a wordless question to her loving friend.

"There's only one thing to do," Emily smiled sympathetically, having learned a good deal during the short ride. "If you are not to take this lying down, you must come out, dear Kate, as you never have, but as you might—with all justice due you. There's not a woman in London could hold a candle to you, if you would allow yourself some . . . some flair!" Perceiving that her friend quite understood her drift, Emily hugged her gently. "Come, we must sleep. We have much to do tomorrow, if you are to take London by storm, and," she brazened, "and Lord Alexander by the tail." She found all the confirmation she needed in the simple fact that Kate offered no rebuttal.

Eight

The following three days involving Kate's refurbishment were to become but a blur for that young woman. Yet, as Emily began to emerge as a benevolent tyrant, so Kate began to understand the intricacies of becoming fashionable—the incredible amount of time, energy, and knowledge needed to insure one's success.

Their first day was spent entirely at the establishment of Madame Phillipa Mayware, that reknowned spearhead of haute couture. Madame Mayware herself had opted to design for Kate after privately conferring with Emily who, along with her mother, had a long-standing friendship with the designer. That great lady had been persuaded to leave her studio to have a "look" at Kate, which she did for three minutes, clucking all the while, after which she agreed the girl to be a most promising figure. That "fortunate" girl was then made to do her turns, to be measured and remeasured, draped and pinned until Madame Phillipa was satisfied as to style, color, and cut of the many fabulous creations she would do for her.

The second day was spent at the milliner's, booter's, and glover's where Emily tirelessly purchased accessories to match Kate's new wardrobe. On the third afternoon, Kate learned the intricacies of London's warehouses—where to find the best quality cloth, and as importantly, how to bargain for it. It was an exhausted young woman who was allowed to rest on the fourth morning, that she might be in shape for the afternoon's final fittings! Eustace was in ecstasy over Kate's refurbishment and swore eternal thanks to Miss Castorham all week long. Of course, Eustace was not told the real reason for Kate's reluctant turnabout, nor did Emily and Kate even actually discuss it, the matter having been easily discerned by Emily "that night," as the meeting with Marguerite, Lord Edward, and the Marquess was now referred to, which it rarely was.

So it was that Lady Eustace could gasp in admiration the night Kate descended to attend Emily's private ball. Ostensibly held to be Miss Castorham's regular rout, it had been secretly designated by that generous young woman to be the scene of Kate's reentry into society. Only the cream of the ton had been invited, which was to be expected, Lady Castorham being a high stickler; but Emily had contrived that "those three," as she called Lord Edward, the Marquess, and Marguerite, be present at her affair. She would keep Kate under wraps until they came and then present her friend, who would be an instant success, she had no doubt.

Out of all this Kate came to appreciate the goodness of Emily, and also to watch the curious and gratifying blossoming of that young woman. Heretofore, Emily had been the quietest of young women, showing her wit and graciousness to only a select number of close friends. Now Emily was beginning to evince greater character, so that while Kate privately bemoaned her own transformation, she was yet sensitive to Emily's parallel transformation. Aware that her friend was' also making a "come-out" of sorts, Kate was grateful to see Emily derive some benefit from what Kate secretly considered a vast waste of energy, time, and money. Not that she ever complained, she would never burden Emily so, considering what the girl was doing for her. But Kate was fretful, and the only thing which silenced her was the memory of that horrible carriage ride. She would do anything to be revenged for the cruelty of Marguerite Charles and the contempt of the Marquess of Landonshire: she had in mind that Emily's ball was to be her Armageddon.

Blessed with great insight, Emily was well able to appreciate the stress Kate was under. She knew her friend felt untried and nervous and had much riding on a public success. She also knew that nothing she could say would alleviate Kate's qualms, not even her own confidence in Kate's incredible beauty. So she gave, instead, what she could give best—her knowledge of what she was about in order to create for Kate a bang-up showcase. If she entertained private ideas about a certain Viscount Edward Brougham, she never spoke of it to anyone, and did not deem it in the least necessary. The only message which passed between the young women had to do with what concerned Kate, and was only expressed in a pause in the day's work, a silent communion of spirit and purpose.

And so, as mentioned, when the evening of Emily's ball arrived and Kate descended the stairs to greet her aunt, that good lady was able to gasp in genuine awe and admiration. Kate was attired in a high-waisted creation of the sheerest black silk which clung to show her exquisite figure to a scandalously dangerous proportion. Her décolletage amazed the aghast Lady Wellington and it was all she could do to avoid a hint of warning. Kate's burnished hair had been brushed till her head ached, and after much discussion betwixt Emily and Agatha, done up in a simple topknot, curls falling wispily to the nape. A single strand of diamonds fell to her waist, as did a strand of the finest black pearls her ladyship had ever seen. "Gracious me" was all Eustace could say, tears smarting her eyes as Kate bent to kiss her cheek.

"Wish me luck?" Kate whispered.

"Oh, my dear girl," Lady Eustace smiled, "you'll carry the evening the moment you are seen!"

Emily had stationed herself at the entrance as a good hostess was wont to do, but stayed later than was customary. Not neglecting her own appearance, but keeping Kate's in mind, Emily had attired herself entirely in white satin trimmed off the shoulders with Italian blond lace which became her no end. At a quarter to ten, her butler announced the last arrivals, and Emily knew the dénouement was about to be played. She held her breath as Lord Edward Brougham entered on the heels of the Marquess of Landonshire, who had accompanied Marguerite Charles and her mother, the stout Lady Charles. Marguerite had opted to wear a satin confection done up in the latest fashionable "rose-of-sharon" pink, which made her look enchantingly youthful. Which was exactly what Emily had hoped for, so making it easier to compliment the chit.

"My dear Miss Castorham," Lord Edward bowed, "you look lovely, simply lovely."

"Thank you, Lord Edward," Emily murmured. "And thank you for attending my ball. So good of you to take the time," and she was pleased at his puzzlement as she turned abruptly to greet her other guests.

"Lady Charles, how do you do? Miss Charles, your lordship."

"A lovely party, Emily," exclaimed Lady Charles agreeably, unusually generous since the Marquess of Landonshire had taken to squiring her daughter. "A most becoming dress. And where are your momma and papa? Oh, yes, I see them. I must make my compliments. Come Marguerite," and she took herself off to greet them, assuming her daughter to be not far behind.

"Miss Emily," Marguerite Charles began, "you

must tell me who your jeweler is. I declare, that's a fine cut you wear."

Not as fine a cut as you soon shall have, thought Emily mischievously. "You're too kind, Miss Charles," she smiled instead and snatched a quick look at the Marquess. Dressed in black broadcloth adorned with Michelin lace at collar and cuffs, he was, she declared, the perfect match for Kate. Taller then she'd expected and far more handsome than she'd known, he made Emily experience a momentary qualm on behalf of Kate. That poor innocent babe and this cousin of the devil! Well, stranger things had happened.

"Tell me, Miss Emily," she was brought back by Marguerite, "have you attended any more strange meetings since last we met? I promise, I've told everyone about it."

"Did you now?" asked Emily quietly. "It's a pity, for Madame Markham is so select," and she was pleased to watch Marguerite pale and essay a second attack.

"And does your little friend so easily gain admission? Oh, I forget, Miss Barrister contrived to bring you," Marguerite sneered, but Edward unwittingly smoothed things over.

"Kate 'little?' " he declared with a laugh, "I don't think I've ever heard anyone call her that. Well-built woman, if you ask me. What do you think, Alex, am I right, or wrong?"

"Yes, well," spoke the Marquess for the first time, a slow smile playing around his lips, "I would not call Miss Barrister a small woman, in any manner of speaking." Then turning to Emily, he continued, "She is not here tonight, I see. But then she does small honor to so noble a friend. I remember how you defended her one night, not so long ago. I thought you were brave, we all gave you both such a difficult time."

Emily blushed at his forthrightness and admired the irony of his choice of subject: the same memory which caused dear Kate such pain came so easily to his lips. "So you did, Lord Alexander," Emily smiled shyly, "and have much to be forgiven. But Kate needs no defense. She is a powerful woman in her own right, and would be the first to deprecate such aid."

"Quite right, quite right," Edward agreed, "she's a woman in the least feminine mold and well able to care for herself. Told me so herself. Once, in passing, I thought we suited, but she was too much for me. Became a regular bluestocking, as it turned out. Could have knocked me over," he smiled broadly and Emily thrilled to his self-complacency.

"Yes," agreed Marguerite, "how very strange it was to see Kate that night. But she was never one for parties, come to think on it. Oh, well, no one seems to miss her." She flashed a smile at the Marquess who seemed to take it in his stride.

"Well, Miss Charles, perhaps you haven't," Emily deftly remonstrated her guest, "but I certainly have, and because I did, I persuaded Kate to attend this ball." There was a slight bustling in the antechamber and the doors suddenly flew open. "I think that's her now." Emily fought back tears of pride as Kate floated into the ballroom, her black gown swirling about her to reveal the beauty Emily knew had always been there. It was the greatest moment of Emily's life, she was later to think, to observe the stunned silence which met Kate's entrance. She sent Kate a wink, saw the girl's lips quiver with suppressed laughter, and knew Kate would do just fine.

"Kate, dear, you look very nice," she carefully understated. "Come, let me introduce you to my guests. Oh, but of course, you know Lord Alexander, Miss Charles, and Lord Edward." Emily paused before entering the ballroom. Marguerite and Edward could only nod dumbly as Kate flashed them a small smile.

"We've met," she said coolly. "How do you do?" They were too overwhelmed to respond. "Marquess," she deftly turned to greet Hallesley who bowed over her hand.

"Charmed," he smiled and took note of the abrupt withdrawal of her hand.

"Gentlemen, Miss Charles," Emily nodded with a grave air, "you must let me make Kate known to my other guests. There are those of us who have missed her during her stay away from society, so busy as she has been on her papa's book. Which is as great a success as I am sure she shall be." Then to her surprise, Kate bent to place a kiss on her cheek before they swept away, arm-in-arm. And it was with great satisfaction that Emily was able to observe from the corner of her eye a small smile playing on the Marquess's lips.

Emily's rout was certainly one of the great successes of the season, second only to Kate's dramatic return to the ton mainstream. People greeted her with a warmth that truly moved that young woman who had previously only harsh words for society. The pleasure it gave her was enhanced by the fact that somehow it had got around that *her* book, as people insisted it be called, had been an unqualified success in academic circles. Although most of them laughingly admitted that they would never read such a swell tome, they yet seemed able to appreciate the labor Kate had put into it, without thinking the less of her. True, some teased her for being a bluestocking, but oddly enough, they seemed to do so with a sense of pride. Kate supposed she made their own lives seem somehow less frivolous, and she allowed that perhaps it might. After all, they didn't snub her and that was a great deal for them, well she knew.

And so Kate and Emily happily danced their way through the evening, their dance cards filled by every eligible in the room. And though they never glanced the way of the Marquess or Viscount, they knew their every movement as surely as they knew of Marguerite's dismay at no longer finding herself the toast of the ball. They were just leaving the supper room when a footman appeared with a message from Eustace requesting Kate join her. As they began to make their way in her general direction, Edward appeared in their path.

"Kate, Emily," he began, "er, Miss Barrister, Miss Castorham, I beg your indulgence." The two women were silent. "Er, ah, lovely ball, don't you think?" He searched for words to break the ice, and unable to find any, sent Emily a mournful plea.

"I shall return in a moment," Kate whispered loudly to her friend. "I think perhaps I am not wanted," and they laughed to see Edward blush most profusely.

Emily eyed the Viscount warily as Kate left to wend her way through the crowd.

"Miss Castorham, I, er . . ." Edward lamely began, only to be silenced by a look from his hostess.

"Lord Edward," Emily sternly began, "I think you owe Miss Barrister and me an apology."

"I, ma'am? An apology?" exclaimed Edward, sincerely confused.

"That's what I said," she continued severely, "for the abominable behavior we were made subject to endure some nights ago, when you saw us home."

"I don't understand . . ."

"Oh, don't you? What a poor friend you are, then—especially to Kate."

Edward huffed and puffed indignantly. "I am the very best of comrades to Miss Barrister. Why, I've known her for years, positively years. Ask her yourself." But his eyes fell before hers. "Miss Castorham, to what do you refer?"

"To your lack of support the night Miss Marguerite Charles and Lord Alexander saw fit to ring a peal over Kate. Never have I been witness to such dastardly behavior. And you, sir, although you did not actively participate, most certainly did nothing to . . . to call a halt to their abusiveness."

Edward was truly horrified. "I had no idea, I swear, this was going on. Why, Miss Charles always shows a nasty side though she's pretty enough to look at. I thought everyone knew that. And as for Alex—well, Alex is . . . Alex! Cold and gruff, but really the nicest of men, once one gets past his bluster. Very upset he was, too, the way Kate shut the door on his face. Talk about ringing a peal!"

Emily's ears pricked up at that last although she dared not betray any interest. "He got what he deserved," she retorted, vaguely wondering just where the Marquess was at that moment.

"Look, I do apologize, sincerely, I do," promised Edward most humbly. "I had no idea . . . I'm a dolt not to have seen. But truly, I meant no harm, and saw none, or I would have rescued Kate. I love her like a sister, and come to think of it, can perhaps be blamed only for acting as a foolish brother might. But I don't suppose you wish to converse any longer with me, so . . ." He bowed low.

Emily finally knew ascendency over a man for the first time in her life, and though she was not by nature mean—and even had some partiality for Edward—she could not help but test her skill. "Lord Edward, you were about to solicit a dance, perhaps, when you first came upon Kate and me?"

"I was."

"Then do so." Emily was pleased to note the confusion spreading over his face.

"Miss Emily . . ."

"Thank you. I will have the pleasure of your company." She smiled wickedly and allowed the poor man to carry her off.

Meanwhile, Kate had made her way to the dowagers' chairs in search of Lady Wellington. Within moments, she had found her seated with the Duke of Landonshire, their heads bent close together in conversation. But the smile on Kate's lips died as she took in the tall figure lounging beside them so disinterestedly, yet feigning attention. Her heart pounded in her ears as she tried to deny the impact he made on her. Perhaps he was the handsomest man in the room, she admitted, but he was the devil's child as well. She strode across the room hoping her legs would carry her, aware that Lord Alexander had noticed her, even seemed to perk up as if he had been waiting. His cold, gray eyes raked her in and Kate paled, angered by his effrontery.

As for the Marquess, he kept his face a mask, but his thoughts were not without substance. Although he had attempted to push any memory of her from his thoughts, Kate's face had repeatedly returned to him any number of times since Christmas. He had even dreamed of her on a number of occasions, which fact distressed him no end. Now, the woman he had insulted so recklessly long ago was making her way toward him, her loveliness leaving him breathless. And the thought which pressed upon him as she approached was that as far as he was concerned, she was completely unapproachable. Then she was at his side and propriety dictated small talk. Alert to the nuances of their relationship, he found the idea absurd, after all that had passed between them, but he knew the rules and played them.

"Miss Barrister." He bowed.

"Your lordship," Kate replied, but there was no warmth in her voice.

He could see she was seriously displeased by his presence, and he supposed she was within her rights, but he determined to keep to civilities. "I would like to offer my congratulations on the printing of your father's manuscript. It is an admirable thing which you have done." He offered an olive branch.

"How kind," Kate responded stiffly.

His brows arched, but he maintained a politic silence and stepped aside as his father rose to offer his own felicitations.

"My dear young lady." The Duke took both her hands and bestowed a kiss upon her cheek while Lady Eustace watched, beaming. "We have just been talking about the successful reviews your book has been garnering. What you have done is no less than brilliant, and I am proud, as your own father would be. You have given historians an important gift and it portends a great future for yourself. You will be one of the great women of this century, I have no doubt, if you continue on as you have. Do not underestimate your own value." He gently shook his head, seeing her self-deprecation. "Remember, I have read the text and know of what I speak. But enough, we shall talk later. Go you and enjoy some champagne. My son looks thirsty also. Perhaps you could take him in hand?" Then he drew Lady Eustace away leaving Kate and the Marquess alone to their own devices. Taking a deep breath, his lordship spoke first.

"My father's effusiveness brings to force the quality of your work. I had no idea, Miss Barrister. I humbly offer my apologies—on many counts, I fear."

"I don't understand, my lord," Kate said, her voice deadly cold.

"I refer to the paramountcy of your achievement. My father is an authority on such matters." Then he sidetracked himself. "Must you 'lord' me all the time? It makes me feel positively ancient—" to which he received a blank stare. "Miss Barrister, whatever else you may believe of me, I am not without any sensibilities!"

"No?" Kate smiled and he understood that she smiled for public reasons. People were beginning to give them sidelong glances and naturally, she would not be unaware. "Shall I introduce you to some of my acquaintance, sir? No doubt they are anxious to meet such a noted Corinthian." He did not miss the scorn in her voice.

"I know that you despise me," Alexander spoke quietly, "and no doubt you have good cause. I have behaved abominably toward you times untold and can only beg to be allowed to truly express my regrets. But you would do well to remember the extenuating circumstances," he added sharply, for he was feeling greatly provoked. "After all, your own behavior is not past blushing for."

"You are a rogue to make any reference to the past." Kate blanched, appalled at his seeming vulgarity.

"How can I not," Alexander exclaimed, oblivious to their surroundings, "when it is the issue at hand?" But suddenly he was not so sure, as he took in this woman dressed in a gown made to break a man's heart. He even wondered vaguely who the man was.

Kate's green eyes positively burned as she turned roundly on him. "The only issue at hand, sirrah, is your provoking manner."

"And yet, a degree of civility on your part would do wonders for the matter," he threw out bluntly, inexplicably hoping for a truce.

"Civility on my part?" Kate spluttered, "oh, if I were a man and could use a pistol, I would shoot you on the instant!" But to her astonishment, Lord Alexander threw back his head and laughed.

"But madam, you forget yourself. If you were a man all this surely would not have come to pass. In any case, a woman can learn to shoot a firearm as well as the opposite sex. If you wish it," he added, eyes glinting provocatively, "I would personally instruct you in the art. Why, if you placed yourself in my hands, I could teach you a great deal in a matter of weeks . . . sooner, if you betrayed any talent," and he wondered at his audacity.

"Lord Alexander Hallesley," Kate gasped, "you know not what you say."

"I suppose that that is a refusal." He pretended a sigh. "Pity, for you seemed such an apt pupil— once, long ago." Immediately he regretted his words. Kate swayed, and thinking she was about to faint, he drew her into the deserted hall. He noticed her hands tremble and it softened his temper instantly. "Forgive me," he began, bent on making a clean breast of the matter, but she waved him aside and moved away.

He crossed to her side and placed himself in her path so that Kate saw only the blue diamond twinkling in the folds of his cravat. She shivered although she was not cold, and he could hardly fail to notice, and misinterpret: "I realize my reputation doesn't stand high in your books, but you must know that I would not harm you." Kate cringed to hear him speak so.

"Look at me," Alexander commanded and it was impossible not to do so. Kate raised her eyes to meet his, fierce pride reawakening, and she determined not to cower before him.

"It appears we are born adversaries, for whenever we meet we are at *pointe non plus*. It also appears that, given our social standing, we are destined to meet from time to time. This seems correct, of late?" He awaited her reply but Kate was beyond giving any response, so he took up the threads to give her breathing space.

"Given these two premises, we must come to some understanding. We simply cannot come to blows each time we meet. People will begin to talk and we'll begin to appear as fools. You and I must call a truce in our little war, or one, or both of us will be seriously harmed. I suggest that our past differences be set aside and our future meetings marked by a discreet silence, in defense to that past. Henceforth, any intercourse should be acknowledged as courtesy demands: a few words concerning one's health, the weather, or some such nonsense will suffice. To be concluded vis-à-vis swift departure by either party. Society will smile upon our acquaintance and we shall smile upon our own good manners. Do you find this proposal satisfactory, or have you a better one?" he inquired gently, his lips pursed in expectation.

"No," Kate answered with a long sigh, having collected herself, "you're perfectly right, we must make our peace. There is no question that we may meet occasionally and cannot continue to spar so. Yes, let us call a halt to this strife we have thrust upon ourselves."

Alexander was taken aback by her unexpected accommodation and viewed it with some cynicism. "It is amiable of you to acquiesce," he parried.

"I have no choice," Kate claimed hurriedly.

He ignored this last, but unfortunately, continued: "We are possessors of unaccountable tempers and it would do well to keep them in check, lest we cause a small scandal."

Kate was at once indignant. "I'm no hoydenish

105

miss to be doing any such thing, I do assure you, sir." She held her head high proudly.

"No?" he snapped back. "Well, you are certainly forward enough every time I meet you!" and he warmed at the thought of their encounters.

Kate stood there, fists clenched, glaring at the Marquess. As Alexander watched her, it came to him at that moment that all his troubles with this hot-tempered woman had but one source, which fact was suddenly revealed to him. His entire body stiffened in shocked response and he felt tongue-tied for the first time he could remember. He was in love, damnation! Why hadn't he seen so from the start? He was in love with the wench. Damnation!

Kate sensed, more than saw, his sudden tension, and felt unaccountably remorseful. Her animosity suddenly melted away and she felt decidedly foolish.

"Lord Alexander, I must apologize," she said softly, laying a hand on his arm. "I'm behaving like a termagant, having blown everything out of proportion. Let us bury the proverbial hatchet. Henceforth, I will follow your advice and keep miles between us, and if ever we do meet, I shall hie the other way. I promise you will be subjected to no more scenes." Her voice broke on her words.

"Kate," Alexander started, unsure how to respond.

"No, milord. Don't say another word." She drew herself up with great dignity. "I could not trust my tongue at this moment. Indeed, it does seem to run away with me whenever I'm in your company." Her eyes filled with unshed tears and she lowered her head, praying he might not see. "I simply don't understand . . ." but she could not finish, and turned, and disappeared up the stairs, before he could know what she was about.

"I love you," Alexander said to the empty air, "that's what you don't understand." But it was too late for Kate to hear.

Nine

For the rest of the season, Kate determined to put the Marquess out of her mind, and to some degree she was successful. This was actually made easy for two reasons. Firstly, she accepted every invitation she could, which left little time for thinking. Secondly, at one of these outings she learned that Alexander Hallesley had left London, destination unknown, for an indeterminate time.

In mid-June, Emily Castorham, under the strict supervision of her mama, threw an al fresco at the nearby family estate at Chiswick. Kate and Lady Wellington arrived punctually, and Kate was immediately carried off by her friend to join in the frivolity. Everyone laughed uproariously when Lord Edward Brougham drove out on little Joseph Castorham's donkey cart and all clamored for a ride. As turns were meted out, Lord Edward was able to draw Kate away for a leisurely walk.

"Kate, dear, you're looking in fine feather these days. That's a fact, bye the bye, not a lazy compliment."

"Why, thank you, Edward." She laughed.

"You certainly are quiet these days. Is there a secret to be had from you?" He teased as he fiddled with some daisies.

"My lord," Kate grinned, more like her old self than even she knew, "if there was, I would certainly not tell."

"You make mock, but I'm concerned, truly I am," he admonished and she stopped to lean against an oak. "You're different. You've changed, I'm sure of it."

"Whatever do you say that for? I'm as amiable as may be," Kate frowned.

"That's just what I mean, Kate Barrister. You weren't so used to be, though you may think it. You did seem to . . . to have more . . . spunk! I know of what I speak, even if you don't. Or won't," he added darkly.

Kate shrugged. "Sir, you're much too serious for a picnic. Let us talk of gayer things. How goes your courtship of Emily? She's a lovely girl and deserving of the best."

"As I hope to offer her," blushed Lord Edward. "With her best friend's permission, of course," he teased.

"Oh, you have it," Kate returned lightly. "But I'm happy for you both," and she gave the blushing man an unexpected embrace as they continued up the path to the house.

"Do you remember how once you wanted to marry me?" Kate smiled as she hooked her arm in his.

"Bless me, of course I do, and it's that grateful I am you wouldn't have me."

"Well, this is what I've been waiting for. Now you know love and I'm so glad it's Emily you have found. She has done me no end of good turns and I also love her dearly."

"Yes, well, now that I'm disposed of," Lord Edward winked, "what about you?" But he was interrupted by a shout from behind and they turned to see Emily racing up the hill to join them.

"Hey! Wait for me," and within moments she was before them, panting to catch her breath. Her jonquil gown swayed with the breeze and a straw bonnet lay on her shoulders, its blue riband still tied about her neck. It was with great pride that Edward took her arm in his free one and escorted both women on.

"La," grinned Emily impishly, "you two seemed so lost to the world I knew the conversation must be deep!"

"Quite," smiled Lord Edward, "I was just inquiring of our friend when we would dance at her wedding party."

Emily blushed delicately, for Kate's sake as well as hers. "Oh, Edward, have you no sense of discretion?"

"Hmph, discretion be ... my foot! Kate's my friend. No need to stand on propriety, eh, Kate?"

"No Edward, of course not." And in answer to Emily's speaking look: "Naturally I made your fiancé no answer, having none to give."

Emily made no comment; having been made

privy to Kate's confidences she knew full well how bleak her friend's future looked. She fought back tears on Kate's behalf, tears over the sentimental and not inconsistent wish that Kate might be as happy as she. Avoiding Kate's eyes, and Edward's especially, that she might not cause undue comment, she was grateful when they reached the house.

"We were just wondering when you young people were going to remember us," smiled Lady Castorham, as the trio came into sight.

"Everyone is trailing behind and should be here momentarily," Edward informed her.

"And how did your jollity come off, young man?"

"I fear that it was such a success that it delays your guests for luncheon, ma'am. Everyone is taking turns on the cart being a child again."

"Well, it was to be expected. When you came round from the stable in that tiny cart, I confess I had the same impulse, so I understand the temptation," Lady Castorham laughed.

"In any case, we were having a comfortable coze," Eustace injected, "and never really minded the time."

"Gossiping, ladies? I hope it's not my character which has been maligned this hour. It has taken me a lifetime to build it up," twinkled Edward.

"No, no," Lady Wellington answered smartly, "no one would do you such an injustice. In any case, we were not tearing anyone's character apart. Lady Castorham was just about to give me news of some old friends, which perhaps may interest you, Kate."

"Yes. You see I live but a few houses down from the Duke of Landonshire, in London. I could not help but know," explained Lady Castorham by way of introduction.

"Pray continue," said Eustace, giving her full attention.

"It's about the Duke's son, actually. The Marquess, Lord Alexander . . ." Lady Castorham clarified and Kate felt her heart skip a beat. "He's gone," her ladyship announced dramatically.

"Gone?" echoed the girl dumbly, "I don't understand." She felt Emily's hand reach for hers.

"Gone," repeated Lady Castorham firmly, "just like that." She snapped her fingers for emphasis.

"Gone where?" inquired Lord Edward, who had not seen any friends of late, so much time had he been devoting to his courtship.

"He left for India yesterday morning. Five trunks piled high on the coach and never a by-your-leave. The Marquess admitted it was unexpected but insisted he craved a change of climate. The Duke looked positively crestfallen, and I'm sure I couldn't blame him."

"It's not possible," gasped Lady Wellington, "it's just simply not possible."

Lady Castorham commiserated. "One does hear tales of disease and violence and such, it's no wonder the Duke is upset. But I do wonder what made Lord Alexander go? I'm sure he didn't mention it last time I saw him. That was at your rout, Emily, was it not?" she turned to her daughter for confirmation.

"Yes, Mama," the girl barely managed to say, "but he said naught of this matter. Not that he would, to me."

"You both talked for quite a while, as I recall, Miss Kate. Did he make mention of any such plan?" Lady Castorham pursued.

"No, he didn't say a word." Kate clung to Emily's reassuring fingers.

Eustace turned back to her friend. "My goodness, this is a surprise. I must call on the Duke tomorrow and see how he does. I appreciate your informing us of this, Millicent. The poor man must be heartbroken," and tears filled her eyes.

"Yes, I quite agree. The Duke and his son went their separate ways, but there was great affection between them. Now the Duke doesn't know when next he will see his son. 'Years,' I understand the Marquess said it might be." She shook her head sorrowfully.

"It's not possible," repeated Eustace, "I am simply stunned."

Alexander Hallesley gone to India, Kate tried to assimilate. Why, in heaven's name? She briefly wondered if it had to do with her, but dismissed such a paltry thought as selfish. Me, she laughed bitterly; people don't leave their country on account of someone they may despise. In any case, she reasoned, they only did so in books, and only in romances, and their relationship could not be called a romance by any stretch of the imagination. More like a war, she remembered sadly, and one of improbable value. Why did he go, she wondered again, and it behooved her to admit that he must have had his own private reasons.

Try as she would, Kate could not shake herself of the lethargy which suddenly overtook her, but she was honest enough to admit (albeit privately) that it directly reflected Lord Alexander's departure. Their entire short history had been marked by disaster, yet the news shook her to the core. She remembered their last meeting, when he had in all likelihood been preparing even then to leave England. What a send-off I gave him, Kate thought, chagrined. A fond memory to take half way across the globe!

"Perhaps it's wanderlust," came a voice, Lord Edward's, recalling her from her thoughts. He also had been taken by surprise, Kate noted, and they had been such good friends.

"Wanderlust, bah," snapped Eustace angrily, "Alex Hallesley is all of thirty. His days of wanderlust have long since gone, his dissolution notwithstanding. There's a woman involved, I'd stake my life 'pon it. This is just the sort of thing that would happen to that handsome, arrogant young pup. To be sure, he has been rejected by some lightskirt and has run away in a temper. Although a woman must needs be touched in her 'upper works' to refuse an offer from him."

"And yet it's hard to conceive Lord Alexander being overset by a lightskirt," Lady Castorham considered. "Perhaps he had developed a more noble tendre and received his notice to quit from that quarter," she suggested. "He's been seen with Marguerite Charles, for instance, if rumor serves me well."

"Lud! Lord Alexander never seriously looked at such a schoolgirl in his life. He wouldn't be bothered with such insipidness, I've ofttimes heard him say," countered Eustace. "I'm sure he was only toying with her."

"Oh, I don't know," Edward began only to be quieted by a look from his beloved. He took himself off indignantly to the lemonade tray, wondering what he had said.

Kate felt herself begin to tremble but common sense held her in check. Marguerite Charles! How could he? Impossible, instinct told her. But the idea had been planted and rankled.

The afternoon dragged on, but was over at last, and Eustace and her niece were able to depart. They rode home in silence, but as their carriage pulled up before their house, Eustace turned abruptly to her niece. "There is a woman involved somewhere, mark my words," she said sadly, "but did he have to fall so hard?" Kate could only stare mutely at her aunt's unspoken appeal for comfort. She knew Eustace loved the Duke and that anything which hurt him pained her as well.

But the sense of loss to herself was that which most compelled Kate to seek the refuge of her room. Sitting by the window, chin resting on hand, she summoned before her the dark face of Lord Alexander. And it was forced upon her, powerfully and emphatically, that the cause of all her distress in connection with that arrogant Marquess lay in the simple fact that she loved him. He had come into her well-ordered life quite by accident and turned everything upside down. And before she had had time to understand her feelings, he had vanished, possibly forever. She felt cheated somehow and could not really blame him, but she did so all the same.

I love him, she cried silently, her tears falling freely. I can't think how it happened, but it has, and now he will never know. And whatever secret had prompted him to leave, it was certainly not me—Kate harbored no false hopes in that direction. Well, at least she knew her own heart, that was something, she supposed ironically. Something to warm her lonely old age, for she knew instinctively that her heart had been given irrevocably, she was that type of woman.

The big season officially ended June 10 with the closing of Covent Gardens. It also customarily ended with a spate of weddings which was, in truth, what the season was about. Generally speaking, there were not many surprises for society kept hawklike watch upon itself, little escaping notice. One or two coups would occur, it's true, but even these were eventually ferreted out.

The morning after the Regent's final ball, Kate and Lady Wellington shared a leisurely breakfast in their private garden, a small plot of land to the rear of the house so well laid as to insure maximum privacy while yet remaining artful. As they sat sipping chocolate, Kate could see that her aunt was inordinately restless. She knew from past experience that an explanation would soon be forthcoming, and so it was after some moments.

"I have told the servants to begin packing the household in preparation for our return to Randomm," Eustace slowly began.

"I can be ready by three," smiled Kate who, if the truth be known, had been ready to quit London weeks earlier.

"I assumed you would be returning home," nodded Eustace, "for you've given me no indication that you entertain alternatives." She hesitated. "Accepting any of those marriage proposals you've received, by way of example."

"No, Aunt, I'm not," Kate returned listlessly, causing her ladyship to send a sharp glance in her direction while Kate only sipped her chocolate, ignorant of the look sent her way.

"What will you do this winter?" Her aunt frowned as she reached for another scone.

"I don't know. Surely write, I think. And then I thought you might want to begin to introduce me to estate management. If I'm ever to be as competent as you, I must begin to be groomed."

"You can also hire a manager, you know. Competent men may be found, if looked for properly. You may not like the work, you see, and your heart must be in it to be of any success."

"You speak sensibly, Aunt, and that's why I wish to try my hand. If I'm not cut out for this work, I want to know, that you might train someone to your liking. I had been thinking, since Papa's book was printed, that this was my next logical step."

"You might marry," insisted her aunt.

"No, really, I couldn't. I would only marry with a man I loved. The thought of anything else fills me with repugnance."

"Yes, well," agreed Eustace who, at the same moment, had turned ever so slightly pink. "That brings me to another matter which I have been reluctant to broach. It's difficult to say but the time has come, and I must have your opinion." She took a deep breath. "The Duke of Landonshire has kindly asked me to consider an offer of marriage." Whereupon her ladyship took a sudden great interest in serving herself more chocolate.

"To whom?" inquired her niece absentmindedly.

"Why, to him, naturally," flushed her aunt, regretting having not better prepared Kate for this news.

"When did all this happen?" asked Kate amazedly. "Only recently did I suspect you might entertain such feelings for each other."

"It happened last evening during the third waltz." Eustace smiled dreamily, then collected her wits. "But actually, it began two years ago. I would not countenance the idea then—you were so young at the time. But as the Duke pointed out only yesterday, another season has just concluded and finds you still in a state of single blessedness. And you've grown some, while I'm not getting any younger," sighed Eustace inaudibly.

Reaching for a scone, Kate contemplated this turn of events, while Eustace contemplated Kate. A vastly becoming woman, she thought, as the sun fell on the girl's golden curls to reveal subtle shades of red. Tall and regal, beautiful and strong, Kate put one in mind of a goddess. Emily had truly done wonders uncovering the natural beauty of her niece. She had always suspicioned how Emily had brought it off and what inducement she had held up to Kate. More often than not a man was involved, but in Kate's case . . . Eustace started guiltily. Even she began to wonder how such a lovely creature could remain unmarried so long.

"Kate, has your heart ever been engaged?" she asked with sudden perspicacity.

"Aunt, I never . . ." Kate stammered, taken completely unawares.

"Is that your answer?"

Kate would not deliberately lie but fierce pride did not allow for complete honesty. She wanted to avoid commiseration as she didn't think she could bear it, however well-intentioned. She also had no wish to detract from her aunt's own happiness, which she felt to be well-deserved.

"All right, Aunt, I was terribly in love once, but it simply didn't work out," she answered, schooling her voice to a lighthearted tone. "I try to forget him, and have succeeded to an extent, but it's hard, you must understand. Please don't worry about me, for it's long past and best forgotten, really. You have found me out." Kate forced herself to laugh. "I hope you will keep my secret."

"Oh, Kate," whispered Eustace, not fooled by Kate's insouciance. But her niece only raised her hands in mock horror.

"Please don't. I want no sympathy, nor words of consolation. It's best forgotten, such old stuff. Pray, no more questions—another time, I beg."

"Surely," acquiesced Eustace sympathetically and leaned forward to take Kate's hand. "But this revelation certainly makes what I have had to say a bit untimely."

"I won't allow you to think it," the girl smiled steadfastly. "Tell me instead what you intend."

"Intend? I don't know! It's tempting, I don't deny. But at my age . . ." Lady Wellington turned away shyly.

"It's true you're older than some, dear Aunt, but consider also, you're younger than others," Kate gently teased. "The only question I wish to ask is if your affections are sincerely engaged?"

"Yes, I think so." Eustace frowned. "Although not in the same way as it was with your Uncle Carelton."

"Well, that's as it should be, for Uncle Carelton was part of your salad days." Kate felt a bit brutal on this point but felt the situation warranted it. "But you haven't answered my question," she persisted. "Do you love the Duke of Landonshire?"

"Yes, I do," Lady Eustace said quietly. "Lord Landonshire says that two such people as we have much to share. He argues that there is still much ahead for us and that it would give him great pleasure to share it with me. For my part, I do not disagree. And he has also enumerated all the names of his friends and acquaintances who re-married at such a late age."

"Bravo for the Duke," Kate cheered.

"Which brings us to my second difficulty: I would become the Duchess of Landonshire. Although there would be no issue from our union, and no real exchange of monies as we are both independently wealthy, I fear people will accuse me of grasping for a title."

"Aunt, no friend who really loves you would harbor such a thought," Kate cried vehemently. "Perhaps you are wise to prepare yourself for such an accusation, for you will probably hear it whispered time to time, but surely you will take comfort in knowing it to be a lie. You must turn to the Duke for his strength at those moments and be solaced, having found such a charming husband. It's what I would do in your place."

Eustace had tears in her eyes as she pressed Kate's hand. "You are wise beyond your years, dearest. I pray every day for your own happiness." And then, abruptly: "But then you are agreed to my marrying the Duke?"

"Did you think I wouldn't be?"

"Not really. And he supposes his own family will not be either. There's only Alexander and his sister, Eloise. She's busy with her own growing family, and quite contented, I understand. The

Marquess can have no fear I will have any children to encumber his patrimony, and besides, he very well might not even return to England." Kate steeled herself against a swell of emotions. His name would obviously crop up in the future so she had best become inured to it, she cautioned herself philosophically.

"The Duke is much distressed over Lord Alexander's departure," continued Eustace, unaware of her niece's discomposure. "He doesn't actually talk about it, but I know he broods. It was grievous ill of the boy to leave and I will write to tell him so myself. When I am married to the Duke," she amended, not wishing to seem pushy.

"Perhaps it's best not to interfere," suggested Kate. "Surely he had good reason for leaving the country. Mayhaps it would be better to find out first, before taking him to task."

"I can't believe any excuse would satisfy the Duke," her aunt insisted, and Kate remained prudently silent. But Eustace's thoughts took an abrupt turn to her original subject.

"There's a fourth difficulty and that is you."

"A fourth difficulty? Me?" repeated Kate, puzzled.

"To my marriage, my dear," explained her aunt.

"Don't give me another thought, Aunt." Kate was emphatic. "I've been thinking . . . it's every woman's dream to be independent, one you yourself have lived. Perhaps it's my turn, and I wish you would agree." She hesitated, then decided to take the plunge: "I would like very much to set up my own household."

"But you're only twenty-five years, not nearly of an age to be independent!" Lady Wellington cried, quite horrified. "I was forty-one when your Uncle Carelton died, and married twenty years. Here I had thought you might come live with the Duke and me after we were married. I do assure you, this offer is from both our hearts, it goes without saying, and was only referring to your being alone for the duration of our honeymoon."

Kate's brows knit in consternation. "I'm sure it does, and I love you both for your offer. But you must understand what an opportunity this is for me. To set up my own household would give me enormous gratification. Oh, don't think me selfish, Aunt, for I love you more than anything, and if you did not support me, I should certainly lead a dismal life. But please, allow me this and surely we would all be completely happy."

"Oh, dear. But what will people say? That I threw you out," cried Eustace, "for the sake of a title! No, they shall say we had a row! Lud, they shall say any number of things!" She wrung her hands fretfully.

"Aunt Eustace, calm yourself." Kate smiled to soothe her ladyship's worries, "I am not going to be intimidated by scandal-mongers, or allow them to run my life. I'm a grown woman, well able to care for myself. Believe me, when time has passed and they see what a humdrum existence I lead, they will concede there is nothing to gossip about."

"And what about fortune-seekers? They will easily take advantage of you."

"Do you think me such a paltry thing as to be so undiscerning?"

"Yes, I do, if the truth be known." Eustace sighed. "You haven't a notion how to get on with men, I'm sorry, my dear, but that's how I see it. You'll end up leg-shackled to an ... an American!"

"La," Kate hooted, "how you do go on. Americans aren't all fortune-hunters, aunt. Besides, I've just told you I don't foresee getting married. But really, if I made my bed you must let me lie in it. If I am such a green goose as you say, well, I shall just have to hope for the best." And then, more softly: "You must let me go, Aunt. I am much too old to be in leading-strings any longer."

"Kate, it frightens me to hear you speak so, but I suppose you will have your way for I am no match for you. Since you are an heiress and an orphan, you could have had your way years ago, and I'm only glad you chose to stay with me. But I admit it's a great thing to be unfettered, and no, I won't stand in your way." Eustace's throat tightened with emotion but she forced herself to continue. "Of course I trust to your staunch upbringing and character, but ..." Kate knelt to embrace her aunt as the good lady caught her breath: "You will promise to summer every year with the Duke and me?" and Kate agreed with alacrity, knowing it would ease her aunt's pain.

Kate had never planned anything so dramatic

for herself but the moment the words were spoken, she knew it to be the right thing. An establishment of her own! Were it anyone else, what a scandal there would be, but she could assure herself on one point: her reputation was secure. Aunt Eustace was right; no doubt a few old biddies would do their mischief, and there might possibly even be a few young ones too, who would let their tongues go awagging. No matter, she would survive them all and live to tell the tale.

If only . . . and the memory of the Marquess of Landonshire forced itself to mind. Kate paled, alarmed by her susceptibility, but it was true—she did still love Lord Alexander and probably always would. An old nursery rhyme popped into her head—how did it go? Ah yes. . . If wishes were horses . . . beggars would ride! Ah yes . . .

Kate shrugged her shoulders and bid the past be gone. Only the future held any importance, and that was not so bad, all things considered.

Ten

1819

It had been two years since the Marquess of Landonshire had strolled down English streets. Old friends greeted him and applauded his return, but it was London itself which chiefly excited him. He was elated to be home and spent much time reacquainting himself with old haunts, familiar landmarks and the general consequence of the city. He had landed quietly at Portsmouth two weeks previous and his first order of business had been to command his manservant to reopen his town house in Portman Square. But in deference to his father, he headed straight for the family estate so as to present himself back in the fold. And indeed, he had been warmly embraced by his father and tearfully hugged by his new stepmama.

"This is wonderful, by all that's holy," the Duke had cried, and Lord Alexander remembered how Lady Wellington's eyes had silently thanked him for returning. (He had been slightly embarrassed by that.) They had insisted he stay for no less than a fortnight, which he really couldn't refuse, admitting to no immediate commitments, nor even distant ones.

On the other hand, he was not averse to seeing how his father got on. It was only four months ago that a letter from the Duke, dated 1817, had found him, and which had informed him of his father's marriage. Now among them, he could easily see, and was relieved to see, that the marriage was a rousing success. It was obviously a marriage of great affection; Lord Alexander envied their serenity and toasted them heartily the first night he was home.

"You've changed, my son," noted the Duke pensively as they all sipped sherry one night. Alexander had smiled but made no reply. "I suppose two years at sea would change any man," his father had continued.

"And seven months in Hong Kong, Papa."

"I know, for I have memorized your letters, grateful that I was to receive all four of them," the Duke could not resist.

"Papa," Alexander grinned, "that was a great many. Jeremiah Creighton did not post nearly so many to his parents."

"Ah, yes, Jeremiah Creighton. The young fellow who stopped you on a street in Firenze and invited you to sail the seas."

"He is a very old friend and utterly trustworthy. It's ironic, but I had almost decided to return to England when I ran into him. Our trip was only to be four months and he was very persuasive, I fear."

"Will we never learn the reason for your leaving London in the first place?" asked the Duke. At which point the new Duchess's ears pricked up, although Eustace instinctively knew she'd hear nothing of great import. She could see that her new stepson had learned well how to keep his own counsel; no doubt there had been times when his life had depended on it.

"No specific reason," she heard him say. "I suddenly tired of England and couldn't get away fast enough. I wanted a change, and must admit I got it," he smiled ruefully. How could he explain the confusion he had been thrown into through the unwitting device of Kate Barrister. Why, even she had no idea of the impact she had made on him—that she'd been the reason he had left England, terrified at the implications of his passion for her. Sitting here now in the intimacy of the ducal chambers and thinking back, it all seemed so childish, the act of a callow schoolboy. Of another lifetime, actually.

"Will you return to society, now you've come home?" Eustace asked. Alexander turned to face her fully, observing the needlework at which she carefully stitched. Eustace smiled gently and quickly bent her head, a head as gray now as the satin gown she wore, and as luminous as her diamond wedding band.

"I don't think I can," returned the Marquess thoughtfully, "at least not to the degree I once did. I've no taste for that sort of flummery anymore, my inclinations having become more placid. I fear I've grown less frivolous."

"I see," mused Eustace. "And are you going to return to London with that monstrous beard upon your face and cause all the ladies to swoon?"

"Ought to shave, if you ask me," opined his father. "Not quite the thing."

"Well, I like it," said Alexander, as he absent-mindedly stroked his whiskers. "We shall see. Indeed, it has been there almost as long as I have been gone and is natural to me now."

"I can see already that your return is going to raise a storm," prophecied his stepmother. "I shall have letters from hysterical mamas complaining how their daughters are languishing for love of the dashing young adventurer lord. You shall be inundated, mark my words, and it will be interesting to see how you get on," she smiled mischievously.

"I'm afraid I'm not all that young anymore," he grinned.

"You know, you must visit Eustace's niece when you return to London. You do remember Kate Barrister? She set up her own establishment also, soon after we were married," the Duke said, oblivious to his son's faint rise of color. This was the first information Alexander had had about Kate since he had left England.

So she had married, sighed Alexander to himself. To Edward Brougham, he made no doubt. Well, after two years he could hardly be surprised. She had been a real charmer, as he remembered, although he gave allowance for memory. Still, it might be interesting to see Kate once again, in light of the fact that he himself had once entertained thoughts about her.

When Alexander finally did return to London his old friend, George Brummell, took him up and arranged his modest reentry into fashionable society. The first time Alexander called on him, that arbiter of fashion took one look at the Marquess's full beard and made his pronouncement: "Outré, Alex! But it stays!" They had then proceeded arm-in-arm to Weston's where Brummell had had the Marquess revamped in the latest styles. And who would know of them better than he? Greatcoats and mantles of broadcloth in only the most muted colors; shirts and cravats of the finest lawn, silk, and muslin; trousers to match all. On to the boot maker and glover, although the Marquess laughingly drew the line when Brummell began to direct his coachman to the haberdasher's.

Eustace was correct in her prediction, for within one week Alexander became the most sought-after bachelor London had seen in over a decade: he was also the most elusive. Although he allowed Brummell to drag him to Almack's once, and attended a number of Prinny's dinners, he accepted no other invitations, preferring to keep his circle small. Yet unbeknownst to him, society being what it was, it was "odds on" at White's which hostess would be the first to entertain him privately. Sally Jersey, unscrupulous woman that she was, had been given the slightest edge, but that fact deterred no one and cards had been left by the bagful, much to the Marquess's chagrin.

Alexander was now off to pay his first formal morning visit and leave his own card, as it were. He had promised to pay a call on Kate Barrister and the idea appealed to him. But he was nervous as a schoolboy, had really been quite difficult with his manservant who had accepted his master's sheepish apology with great curiosity. He had gone off in a hurry, only to tool his phaeton around Hyde Park for twenty minutes before being able to summon up the courage to continue. Eventually he was knocking at Kate's door and being eyed aloofly by her butler.

"Madame is indisposed and seeing no visitors this morning," the elderly man informed him coldly. "If you would perhaps like to leave your card . . ." he broadly discouraged entry.

"Thank you," frowned Alexander, quickly proffering his card, at once relieved, yet vastly disappointed.

"A moment, my lord," the butler smiled, "I had no idea who you were. A thousand pardons, and may I welcome you back to England, if I may be so bold? Madame is in the garden and will surely be pleased to see you. Perhaps you would like to surprise her? She is quite alone, I do assure you, catching up on her letters," he advised.

Alexander gave him a startled look. "Why, many thanks. If you would point the way," and he proceeded as directed. He came quietly upon Kate and stopped to absorb the scenario, which bore a remarkable resemblance to the dreams he had cherished on his travels. Kate was comfortably seated beneath a shady maple, intent upon her letters. A China crepe scarf fell from one shoulder while her unpinned hair cascaded down to her waist, reminding him of other days. Alexander's heart constricted and he wondered (not for the first time) how he had let her slip through his fingers. Kate lifted her head and he could not help but smile at the faraway look in her eyes. Instinctively, she sensed a presence and turned to look about. She found him out at once and he watched as a full range of emotions flitted across her face. He wondered what dreams he had interrupted.

"Your butler was kind enough to point the way." He spoke softly by way of introduction.

"It's a pleasure to see you once again, my lord," Kate smiled hesitantly, then held out her hand in salutation. She'd many times fancied the Marquess's return but had never imagined anything this mundane.

"I hope I'm not interrupting, or that we need stand on ceremony, given our new familial status." He bowed awkwardly over her hand.

"No, of course not. I was just woolgathering." She lightly blushed, for indeed she had been dreaming about him! "It's quite charming of you to pay me a call." Kate caught the allusion to his father's marriage with her aunt. Feeling vaguely disappointed, she was yet able to smile. "London talks of nothing these days but the elusive Marquess of Landonshire who refuses all invitations. How fortunate I am; this will elevate my stature no end." Kate's hand flew to her lips, so shrill did she sound to herself. Unable to continue, she could only gaze helplessly at the Marquess, who looked so terribly handsome with a beard, his gray eyes more brilliant than ever.

Unfortunately, Alexander was only cognizant of his own nervousness and took umbrage at her words. "You make me sound a prize bull. I simply didn't want news of my return published abroad, wishing to renew acquaintances at my own pace." He bristled.

Kate winced to hear herself referred to as an "acquaintance" but understood it could hardly be otherwise. "Of course, I quite understand." She smiled gently.

"Do you? But of course—the grapevine. Then you will have heard that George Brummell has revised my itinerary. Naturally, I did not intend that you should be unacquainted with my return. Our being relatives of a sort," he floundered.

"Not at all," Kate murmured, at a loss how to respond. Something was wrong, she sensed instinctively.

Which fact Alexander also perceived, and misconstrued. Assuming that their being even remotely related offended Kate, he was annoyed, although he remained outwardly at ease. "You're looking lovely as ever," he began again, striving for an offhand manner. Truly she was, he thought, much chagrined.

"And you are looking as if travel suited you,"

Kate responded lamely, searching for conversation only to find her wits deserting her.

"My parents convey their best wishes," the Marquess attempted to fill the breach, "and look forward to seeing you in July. I understand you summer at Landonshire."

"Yes, I have these past few years. It's so beautiful there. Did you know your gardens were done by Capability Brown? Indeed, they are a treasure."

"No, I didn't. My mother handled that domain. I suppose the new duchess will want to make a few changes."

"Do you have any objections?" Kate asked delicately, alert to the defense of her aunt.

"Honestly, I could care less," the Marquess replied, sincerely disinterested.

"And how do you like your new stepmama?" she pursued, somewhat curious.

"Oh, quite well. Eustace seems to suit my father perfectly. But if she didn't," he shrugged, "well, it would be nought to me. She doesn't affect me except in the most social way."

"I don't understand." Kate worried at his cold lack of enthusiasm. (She had thought it a splendid match!)

"Well—" His lordship hesitated, a small smile on his lips. "She increases my social circle."

"Oh, yes?"

"Yes! For instance, I may depend on your visiting Landonshire, every now and then?" He was hopeful, but sounded bemused.

Kate mistook him and blushed furiously at his apparent cut. How he must yet despise her after all these years! "Actually," her voice quavered, "I had thought to spend this summer elsewhere." She attempted to salvage her position.

"Oh," responded Alexander, disappointed once more.

"No, really, I had thought to spend the summer with Emily . . . Castorham, as you knew her. She married my good friend, Edward Brougham. They await the birth of their first child."

"Yes, I know. I've been to see them. Edward was a good friend of mine also. Little Emily, a mother." Then, incredibly thoughtlessly, but he couldn't resist: "How came she to marry your lover?"

Kate colored visibly. "He was never my lover, sir, but you would ever insist he was."

"It seems to me—" Alexander frowned, then bit back his words. "How rag-mannered I am, to be sure," he smiled apologetically. But the damage had been done, the atmosphere more strained than ever.

Kate took a deep breath and counted to ten. "Do you mean to stay in England, my lord?" she asked, admiring the idiocy of her conversation. Really, this visit was beginning to contain elements of a farce. Starting to feel decidedly foolish, she began to nurse the hope that he would soon leave. She'd rather resume their conversation when she felt more in control, which she decidedly did not at that moment.

"Yes, I do. I've reopened my house in Portman

Square and am in the process of refurbishing it. My tastes have changed. I require greater simplicity, and to be honest, am heartily glad to have seen the last of the sea."

"Sea, my lord?" Kate echoed, knowing little of his travels, having never had the courage to inquire.

"Seas, I should say. The Pacific, Atlantic, even the Sea of Japan. I've been almost a year in Asian parts and I'm glad to be on English soil once more."

"It must have been terribly exciting." She encouraged him, on tenterhooks to hear more.

"I suppose so," returned Alexander, distracted by Kate's golden glow of enthusiasm. His thoughts wandered, gravely shocking his conscience, and he recalled himself to concentrate only on her words.

The conversation continued in such disjointed fashion for upwards of fifteen minutes. But the Marquess could no longer think, and Kate was fast developing a headache, his visit quite taxing her nerves. There was no question, a more miserable pair would not be found in London that day. Eventually Alexander rose to leave.

"Must you go so soon?" Kate asked politely.

"Er, yes, Brummell awaits me at White's and you know how he is about appointments." He bowed once again and wasn't surprised at the coldness of her touch. She is a cold fish, he told himself, angry at how the interview had gone (or not gone, so to speak) and anxious to blame anyone but himself.

Perhaps he was fortunate, now he thought on it, not to have been caught in her net so many years ago. Yes, his travels were timely, he congratulated himself, no matter how pretty her eyes were! "When you write to my parents, do send my love; I'm notoriously poor at letter writing."

"I shall convey your message, my lord," Kate promised, falsely sweet.

"Now, that will not do for you to 'lord' me so, now we are family," he smiled, feeling very brotherly now that he no longer felt loverlike. "Why don't you call me Alex, as my friends do?" he suggested.

Kate stammered in confusion. "Oh, my lord, I mean, sir, I mean . . . you are kindness itself. But I couldn't, not in my position. It might create its own kind of gossip and I must be circumspect."

"In your position? I don't understand." Alexander frowned. "Have you married a tyrant?" he demanded, sure he was at the heart of the matter. Then he shrugged his shoulders philosophically; he trespassed, and it was not his business, after all.

Kate was incredulous. "Married a tyrant?" she echoed, at a loss as to his meaning.

"Lord help me," apologized Alexander, "there go my manners again. A thousand pardons. I'm sure your husband is the very best of fellows and I'm sorry not to be able to meet him. Another time, perhaps, if you would allow me to call again. Pray, do give him my excuses," he begged and Kate only nodded as he hastily turned on his heels to leave. If he stayed any longer God only knew what else he would say. But as he passed through the door, he was sure he was not mistaken: the sound of Kate's laughter drifted to his ears.

Eleven

"Please advise her ladyship that I have come for a short visit, if she is well enough to receive." So Kate addressed the butler of the Viscountess, Lady Brougham. He was gone but moments when he returned to show her upstairs. Emily, being enceinte, was not receiving at all times, and when she was, preferred to do so in her private sitting room. Her husband complained good-naturedly that the house ought to be done up in Holland covers, so little did his lady visit its other parts. Huge with child in this last awkward stage of childbearing, Emily would only smile lazily and shake her head. On this day Revson showed Kate up to her friend's private chambers where she found Emily daydreaming over a book.

"What," smiled Kate, as she stooped to buss her friend, "not knitting, not crocheting?"

"I've accepted defeat graciously," Emily grinned, "and given it up. I'm simply no good at it. Odd, isn't it, how a well-bred English girl like myself cannot master the feminine art of stitchery ... and not care! Though I don't breathe a word to

Edward who is good enough to praise even my most glaring disasters!" Emily twinkled.

Kate laughed. "Surely you underestimate yourself?"

"No, not really, I threw in the towel so to speak, last Tuesday, when I discovered I'd knitted three arms for baby's dressing wrap. Tsk, tsk." Emily fluttered her lashes mockingly. Then, in a conspiratorial whisper to Kate: "I hated the dratted thing, anyway!"

It was all Kate could do to keep her seat, so hard did she laugh. Emily rang for tea as Kate collected herself. It arrived in moments, wheeled in on a silver caddy, and Emily waved her maid a dismissal so as to be more private with her friend.

"Emily, I've got to talk to you." Kate took a deep breath. "I've seen the Marquess, Lord Alexander. He paid me a morning call yesterday."

"He visited? What an honor that is," Emily exclaimed, "given how he's been refusing invitations left and right. He has been to see Edward once or twice this past week, but I didn't have a chance to tell you."

"What did you think?" Kate tried for an offhand tone, which Emily understood and allowed to pass unremarked.

"Oh, he looked marvelous, don't you think? So handsome in his beard, so romantic-looking, so mysterious, so . . ."

"Do hush, Emily," Kate curbed her friend's enthusiasm abruptly. "I do see your point."

"I'm sorry, Kate." Emily blushed. "But don't you agree?" She peered at her friend.

"Oh, mm, yes," Kate busied herself with pouring tea from a beautifully chased silver urn. "Oh, Emily," she suddenly cried, putting down her cup with a clatter, "he was quite dreadful, quite dreadful, you know. So high-handed and arrogant. Oh, he said such things." Her hands flew to her cheeks.

"What things, dear Kate?" Emily prodded, greatly perturbed. "He is usually the soul of discretion."

"Well, I suppose he might think he was. No." Kate frowned. "He couldn't possibly, he did go on so."

"Kate, you're not being coherent," Emily gently chastized. "Exactly what did Lord Alexander say?"

"Emily, the moment he walked in I felt his condescension. The very first thing he said was that he only visited because," Kate faltered, "because his father married my aunt! He even admitted to having asked them—how did he put it—not to publish his return abroad. He said he wished to renew 'acquaintances' in his own good time. He certainly categorized me!"

"But Kate, you didn't exactly part the best of friends."

"That is not at all the point," Kate explained testily. "He was so brutal about it! If he felt that way, he simply oughtn't to have visited."

Emily sent her a consoling look. "True. But

then, he would have been committing a faux pas. After all, you are kin . . ." ·

"A little less than, if you get my drift," Kate threw out bitterly but was startled to see Emily throw back her head and laugh.

"Alas, even your originality deserts you," Emily said and Kate was forced to smile.

"But there's more. He accused Edward, poor innocent Edward, of being my lover. My old lover," she hastily amended, seeing Emily pale.

"My, my," Emily breathed deeply. "It certainly sounds as if he went after you with a vengeance. Poor Kate! What did you say? What did you do?"

"Say? Do? What would you have me?" Kate hissed at the memory. "I denied it, of course, in no uncertain terms, but he didn't believe a word I said. The viper, the monster."

"You don't mean to say you took this lying down?" Emily cried aghast.

"But of course I did," Kate began to laugh hysterically. "I was so shocked I couldn't think fast enough. He caught me completely off guard and the interview went from bad to worse." She dabbed at her eyes with a bit of lace and peered at her friend dismally.

Emily sat in great consternation, wondering at the tale she was hearing. She found it hard to believe that Lord Alexander would so misuse her friend, so gentle did he seem whenever she met him. She even wondered briefly if the tale was accurate, then gave herself a mental shake: Kate was not given to exaggeration. "Is that all?" she asked, holding her breath, hoping to have heard the worst.

Kate laughed, beginning to see the humor of the situation, and took her friend's hand. "You're so good to listen to me, Emily, especially when you have so many other things to worry over."

"Pshaw, Kate, what fustian you talk. Tell me all. I haven't been so diverted in months. Does it get worse? I can't possibly imagine. Oh, it does, I can see it in your eyes."

Kate's distress was obvious even though she was making a valiant attempt to leaven it with humor. "Worse? Yes, indeed. He thinks . . . I am married!" Emily was thunderstruck. "Don't ask me how for I simply do not know. Or why, or anything! Only that he does, and to a tyrant, for some reason." The room was silent as the women took this in.

"He has lost his wits," Emily finally clucked as she made to refresh their teacups, insisting Kate partake of a biscuit. "It will lift your spirits and you must keep up your strength. This matter deserves no little thought. We simply can't let it alone." She served herself a cucumber wafer and nibbled absentmindedly.

"You know," Kate began slowly, calmer now than when she arrived, "every meeting I've ever had with the Marquess has led to some sort of discombobulation. I wonder why that is."

"Perhaps because you love him?" Emily suggested softly.

"No," Kate returned calmly, "I admitted to that

a long time ago. No, it's more than that. We clash too often, too violently, at times."

"Oh well, as to that, there certainly are variances between your characters, added to which, a great deal of pride, and that always helps to muddle things. You're both so terribly different, it's a wonder you are attracted to each other, and no wonder the affair doesn't flourish."

"He doesn't love me," Kate refuted disdainfully, "why, he doesn't even like me, Emily."

"Now, there you are out. I think he has loved you from the very beginning. No, don't make faces, Kate. And I'll tell you something else: I'll bet my last pound you're the reason he left England two years ago!"

"Emily, how can you say so? You build my hopes—no, I take that back, you don't. But you're right about one thing—I myself wonder that I'm attracted to such a one. So autocratic, so assuming, so . . . oh, I don't know!" She leaned back with a great sigh.

Emily gazed at her friend severely. "You're always going on about what you ought to do, or should feel, or would think. One can't help these things, Kate, and for a very wise woman you are quite silly not to realize this. It will cause you continuing unhappiness not to change your ways and give in to your feeling."

"My goodness, Emily, what a passionate plea," Kate laughed uncomfortably.

"I mean it."

"Yes, I can see that you do. But surely you don't

suggest I liken myself to the type of woman Lord Alexander chases about. I could never pull that off, nor would I wish to. What, then, are you hinting at?" she asked curiously.

Emily could hardly suppress a smile at her friend's innocence. For all the transformation Kate had undergone—her hair, her clothes, even setting up her own establishment, underneath Kate remained as socially unimaginative as the day she was born. There wasn't a flirtatious bone in her body. True, she was capable of being molded—therein lay some hope—but she would waste time on elementary talk. Well, she, Emily, would show her the way. Putting one long, tapering finger to her cheek, she cocked her head at Kate. "I don't ask you to change all that much, dear, only to learn a bit of the gentle art of persuasion."

"To what end?" Kate asked, thoroughly confused.

"Why, the persuasion of Lord Alexander to your side, of course. Now, when did you say Lady Sefton's ridotto was?"

"I didn't."

"Well, never mind, Edward will know the date. Now do have some more tea. We have much to talk about. Unfinished business, as it were." She sent her friend a mysterious smile. "Yes, very unfinished, now I think on it."

Unbeknownst to the women, in another part of the house, Lord Edward also sat entertaining. In a library lined with books only read occasionally, but dusted often, he offered cognac to the Marquess of Landonshire.

"I can't tell you how pleased I am to have you back," Lord Edward was saying. "It's been dashed dull without you these last two years, Emily not included, naturally."

"She's an angel, a paragon," Lord Alexander smiled, accepting a snifter with delight. It was pleasing to be here in this cozy home among his happily married friends—there were so few about these days. He frowned into his drink, which act was not lost on Edward who pounced immediately, not having quite yet mastered delicacy from his wife.

"What is it, Alex? You've been preoccupied all day. I saw it was so over luncheon at White's, and again at Tattersall's. You lost a choice purchase there today not snapping up that mare, but your heart wasn't in it, I could see. Never saw you so wishy-washy in my life. Should have bought her up myself, if old Macroon hadn't grabbed her when you left off bidding. Should have warned me, old boy, but never mind. I say, has anything happened to upset you? Though I don't see what could, only been home a few weeks. But perhaps you want me to mind my own business?"

Lord Alexander laughed at this mouthful from his garrulous friend. "Are you finished, Mister Come-to-the-Point? Do you need another cognac?" Lord Edward took this unflinchingly, used as he was to his friend's roundaboutations.

Lord Alexander shook his head. "It's nothing. Just being back in England . . ." he stroked his beard absentmindedly. "It's been somewhat unsettling to my constitution."

"So I supposed," Lord Edward mumbled and waited expectantly.

"Well, it's like this," Lord Alexander turned a sardonic face to his friend. "When I traveled, I didn't have much to think about except where to go and how to survive. Oh, I saw a great deal, and learned even more, but now it's over." He floundered. "And here I am safely back in the bosom of the Commonwealth."

"And?" prodded Lord Edward.

"Well," sighed the Marquess, "that's just it. I've no longer any need to go about as I did. Nothing compels me, you see. Damned if I'm not bored!"

"Ah," smiled Lord Edward knowingly and replenished their drinks.

"Ah?" mocked Lord Alexander, "I bare my soul to my nearest and dearest and all you can say is 'ah?'" He downed his cognac in one gulp and waved the decanter away.

"What I meant was, I understand."

"Then you have a cure for my malaise?"

"Marriage," Lord Edward announced with great authority. "It cures everything."

Lord Alexander grinned wickedly. "Sounds mighty drastic, don't you think?"

"Not at all, not at all," winked Lord Edward. "It absorbs all one's free time, don't you know. What with sitting in the House of Lords, seeing to my estates, and tending to Emily—why, there's hardly time to be bored. And truly, I'm the happier for it.

Always did want to be married. Why, I was after anyone to marry me, at one point. Dashed lucky not to get leg-shackled before I met my sweet. Not that she doesn't have her own ideas. Gets them from Kate, I suppose. But still, we deal famously together."

At the mention of Kate's name, Lord Alexander's ears pricked up, but he was careful to hide any telltale sign of his interest. In the most off-hand tone he brought forth: "Speaking of that lady, I paid a call on her yesterday. She's a relation now her aunt has married my father, only we couldn't determine quite how."

"Dear Kate. If it wasn't for her, I would never have met Emily. I was after her to marry me for the longest time but she'd have nothing of me, of course. What a fool I was hounding her so. I must have been quite a cross to bear, and so I told her once; she was an angel about the whole matter."

Lord Alexander absorbed his every word as if to save it for future reference. "Angel? Why sir, do you call her that?"

"Well, she could have married me, you see. Taken me up on my offer. But she knew it wasn't what you'd call true love, and had the wits not to settle for less. For that alone I am grateful," Edward explained seriously, and looked up to see his friend staring heavily into the empty air.

In truth, Lord Alexander had gone back into the past, when only moments ago he had complained so bitterly of the future. He was remembering a night that seemed centuries past, when he had found Kate in the arms of his friend. He remembered quite clearly the terrible accusations he had flung at the poor girl, now revealed to him as unjust, as she had protested they were. And which protests he had scorned mercilessly. There were two fools now sitting in Edward's library, he sighed inaudibly, though he'd die before he'd admit it. He was brought up by the sound of his friend's voice and caught at the last few words, something about his visit to Kate.

"How did it go?" the Marquess repeated the question. "You may well ask. We did not get on, sir, we most certainly did not get on. She's the most provoking creature alive, I swear it, and has been since the day I first laid eyes on her." Then, to Edward's undying amazement, the well-traveled adventurer blushed to the tips of his ears. "Never mind." Lord Alexander fended off questions. "Take my word for it, we do not mix well."

Lord Edward was greatly puzzled but dared not push his friend. He had apparently stumbled into deep waters, or at least thought he had, for with Alex one could never be sure. The man was open as a book for the most part, but he had a way of being prideful, and when he was, there was no talking to him. "As you say. Never mind. I'll find you another to wife. Though you'd have made a dashed good-looking couple," and he hardly noticed Lord Alexander blanch as he made to refill their snifters.

What was this? Kate not married? Could he have misunderstood? But she'd said so, hadn't she? Or had she? Well, his father had said so. Damnation, what had his father said? Lord Alexander couldn't remember, so stunned was he by Lord Edward's revelation.

"What a to-do there was when she set up on her own. Of course, she's a very independent thinker, you know. Rather a bluestocking, don't you agree? But she wouldn't have it—living with your father and her aunt, I mean, and there was no one to stop her. Most of her friends supported her though, and things quieted down soon enough."

"Edward, what are you taking about?" Lord Alexander cried, confused beyond endurance.

"I'm talking about Kate," Lord Edward explained in an injured tone, "Kate Barrister, my dear fellow. How about the time she set up her own establishment. Let's see, over two years, now. About the time you left for Burma, or the Indies, or wherever it was you went."

"Venice, actually, at first."

"In any case, Kate set up on her own and that was that. Became a smashing success, naturally, but she didn't seem to care for that. Toned down, after awhile. Very circumspect. Got to be, in her position, I suppose."

"That's quite what she said," Lord Alexander murmured, more to himself than to Edward. "The heavens save me from myself."

"Say what?"

"Never mind."

"Damme, Alex, if you aren't the outside of enough today!" Lord Edward was tolerant only to a point.

"My apologies," Lord Alexander rose hastily to leave. "I agree, I have been a boor. Worse, if you must know, but that's all I can say for now. You're a good friend to put up with me, Edward."

"Are you going? I was just going to ask you to dinner. Emily will be disappointed, Alex. You must know I didn't mean to ring a peal at you."

"Of course, of course, but really, I'm engaged to dine with Brummell and the Prince. But I'll be back," he smiled, "I've heard about your Belgian cook, my friend."

Edward grinned broadly. "One of Emily's brainstorms, I fear. And too successful, by far." He patted his paunch. "I fear to grow as big as she. Well, then, shall I see you next at the Sefton's ridotto?"

"Yes, yes, I suppose," agreed Lord Alexander, anxious to make his way home to sort out what he had learned. "My love to your wife."

"I'll tell her so. And see what I can do for you," he added with a twinkle.

Lord Alexander almost missed his meaning, then grinned behind his beard. "Oh, I don't know. I might come to something yet," he said mysteriously, leaving behind an exacerbated friend.

Twelve

Lady Sefton's ridotto was to be most selectively attended, and Lord Alexander had promised to be there, Kate well knew. Although she had seen him twice since he had paid his morning call, he had never given her more than a passing nod. No doubt he still thought she was married, Kate surmised, marveling for the hundredth time at such misinformation. Well, she would enlighten him tonight; he would not be allowed to pass her over so easily. She was determined to confront him at any cost and not only due to Emily's promptings.

As she entered Lady Sefton's several heads turned in Kate's direction, and she smiled to remember her maid's warning: "There's trouble tonight, miss—make no mistake, you going out half-naked like that. 'Tis a scandal, to be sure, and the Duchess will have my head when she hears, I make no doubt!" A gown of azure sarcenet lay discarded on Kate's bed. In its stead, she had donned a pale peach crepe trimmed with diamante at the breast, deeply flounced in the skirt, and which revealed more than she was generally used to. Diamonds hung from her neck and earlobes, and her hair had been allowed to curl in wisps to frame her face in a most gentle fashion.

As she gave over her wrap to Lady Sefton's maid, Kate was surrounded by a host of eligibles. Yet Lord Edward Brougham still managed to wade through the throng and gain some attention. "Kate, m'love, this is indecent. You will be a most unpopular lady tomorrow if any of those envious mamas have their way."

Kate shot a look past the numerous male heads surrounding her to see that she was indeed the object of some discussion. Apparently the mamas of a few not-so-attractive debutantes were shaking their heads at the attention she was receiving. She smiled up at her friend. "Thank goodness this doesn't happen too often!" Then she took his arm and let him lead her away.

"Emily bid me look after you, but perhaps I will have to fight for the honor, eh?"

"Mayhaps you will," Kate grinned. "But that's neither here nor there. Where is Emily tonight? Is anything wrong? Is she restive?"

"Yes, yes, that's it. She didn't think she could sit through the concert. She tells me to say 'good luck.' Did she mean the music would be so bad? She knows how I can't stand bad music." Kate laughed as she followed him to secure seats, studiously avoiding his eye, which fact he noted, surprisingly enough.

"What are you about? Something's afoot tonight."

He caught at her nervous bearing. "I can tell these things, my dear. Take that gown, for instance: gorgeous though it is, well, I can only say I certainly admire your courage." He pressed her hand affectionately. "I'm glad to see you can still blush. There, there, I won't pry. But Emily will question me no end, you understand, when I return home. Emily! Is she involved in this scheme? No, don't answer that!" But he peered at Kate's face for his answer. "Females! I should have known something was afoot when she insisted I come tonight," he grumbled as they found seats in Lady Sefton's conservatory.

Just then, one of Kate's admirers approached them with champagne and the conversation was discreetly steered to other channels. They were laughing quietly when Lady Sefton came upon them, the Marquess of Landonshire by her side. Dressed entirely in black but for a froth of lace at the throat, the bearded Marquess looked devastatingly handsome. Lady Sefton was looking very satisfied to be seen with him in attendance, and Kate, in all fairness, could not blame her.

"Kate. Edward. You have found each other. How charming to be sure," Lady Sefton observed, eyes glinting mischievously. "What a constant couple you both once were. I can't understand how you never made a match, for it seemed quite imminent at one point. But there, you can never tell how matters of the heart will go, as I'm fond of saying to Lord Sefton."

"Quite true, madam," coughed Lord Edward

delicately, "you can never tell these things. But here I am happily married with nary a regret. I shall tell Emily you wished her well," he thrust pointedly and Kate marveled at his courage for facing up to such a formidable social notable. Stealing a sidelong glance at Lord Alexander, she was disconcerted to find him staring down at her. She paled under his severe scrutiny, momentarily regretting her brazen attire, then rallied herself to flirt outrageously, according to Emily's exhortations.

"Lord Alexander, Lady Sefton, won't you take some champagne?" She beckoned to a nearby footman.

"Edward, where's Lady Emily?" inquired Alexander, faintly ignoring her while yet helping himself to a glass. "I had looked forward to a chat with her."

"She's home feeling too cumbersome to go about tonight. Methinks I'll be taking her down to Crimshaw very soon. That's where she belongs, coming so close to her time. The doctor says, well . . . I won't bother you with what he thinks." Lord Edward caught himself with a grin.

"And a good thing too," snickered Lady Sefton, "or I'd tell my own stories, and you know how I can go on. Take your gown, for instance, Kate Barrister: Now I could go on about that! It takes a certain panache to wear such a dress, but then, you always were eccentric, my dear," her ladyship drawled as she turned to her partner. "Don't you agree she's eccentric, Alex?" Kate paled at such want of tact.

"Madam," he bowed coldly, "Miss Barrister's attire, or lack thereof, is not of immediate consequence."

Kate froze! He had called her "Miss"—then he knew she was not married! Now that was of immediate consquence! Well, there went Emily's plans. But Kate had no time to think as Lord Edward unexpectedly came to her rescue.

"Hear, hear, Alex! Kate looks ravishing and you know it. Why, she puts every woman in this room to shame." Kate's mouth almost dropped in grateful astonishment.

"Sirrah; you are to the point." Lady Sefton laughed, her spangles shaking with her. "But you are right, of course. Kate is in ravishing looks tonight, and I'm a jealous old woman not to admit it."

"Of course I'm right," Lord Edward grumbled, annoyed at both of them, but especially because he could not comprehend Lord Alexander's cavalier treatment of Kate. "I was going to ask you to join us for the concert, but if my beautiful Kate is so hard on your eyes—why, you must just take yourself elsewhere, Alex." Whereupon Kate put a hand to his arm to remind him of their surroundings that he might not make a scene. Why, she sighed to herself, why, oh why, was she always involved in a scene whenever the Marquess was around?

"No, he can't take himself elsewhere," Lady

Sefton interposed, "the musicians are taking their seats and I must tend to my other guests. I've ignored them far longer than I should for the sake of this handsome gadabout." Lord Alexander cocked a brow, which amused Lady Sefton greatly. "You never enjoyed being teased, did you Alex? I'll make amends," she whispered loudly. Then, to Lord Edward and Kate, who had watched this last exchange with interest: "Forgive my high spirits, won't you? Oh, there's my Lord Sefton giving me looks. Enjoy yourselves, do." And she hurried away.

"Hmph," Lord Edward was heard to say as he watched the Marquess take a seat on Kate's other side, but at a look from Kate he buried his nose in his program.

Kate shivered nervously as she obliquely observed the Marquess position his chair. She prudently remained silent. Let him make the first move, she counseled herself; at least that would enable her to retain some slight advantage. He was not long in doing so. Kate felt his breath ever so lightly upon her shoulder as he turned to face her profile.

"Edward is right," he whispered only for her ears, "you do look wondrous tonight, Miss Barrister." Kate was so nervous she could only clutch at her fan, but her program slipped to the floor. As she bent to retrieve it, so did the Marquess, who caught her outstretched hand in his own. "I'm so glad you have no husband to encumber me whilst I take you to task," he sneered. "I refer, of course,

160

to your letting me send my regards to your 'husband,' that morning I visited." They rose, but he refused to release her hand. "Did you laugh a good while, at my expense?" His eyes were cold and guarded, giving Kate no gauge with which to measure his displeasure, but she deemed an explanation timely.

"I, sir?" Kate whispered haughtily, "why, I did nothing! You did most of the talking, and all of the assuming. Your lordship never gave me a chance to explain. A common failing, I'm afraid. Even your abrupt departure was in keeping with your character." Kate was in no mood to forbear. She was thankful to observe the musicians approach the podium, for that at least portended a short conversation.

"Common failing? What do you mean?" Lord Alexander bridled.

Kate was indignant. "Why, the very first time we met you assumed I was a servant, and thereby assumed I was free game. When you found I was not a servant, you assumed I was . . . a flirt! Upon returning to London a few weeks ago, you took it into your head that I was married, to 'my old lover,' perhaps? In all the instances you acted high-handedly, and with great condescension, I might add. And were completely unapproachable, as far as explanations were concerned. You sir, are a boor!" she rapidly concluded, feeling very well-satisfied with herself. "And please do release your hold, sir." She was secretly relieved that he did so.

"To tell the truth," the Marquess threw in unexpectedly, "I did not wish to meet your 'husband.'" But Kate was unwilling to take his hint.

"Well, there is no husband, so you may rest content," and then flippantly, contemptuously: "But if married women are your cup of tea, I do see Lady Valentois. You may remember her as Marguerite Charles. Oh, yes, I see that you do. I can reacquaint you, though we hardly speak. She married an Earl, a bit older than she, but very understanding, I hear tell," and she watched her thrust go home as his eyes narrowed. He would probably love to strangle her, but she figured it was all worth it; she was settling many old scores with him tonight.

"How dare you be so impertinent?" Lord Alexander hissed in a low voice, "you ought to be thrashed, shameless woman. Who was the fool who allowed you to set up on your own? Why you've no more sense than . . ."

"Enough!" Kate whispered furtively, and wished the musicians would hurry. "Who set you up as a social arbiter? Why, your reputation precedes you everywhere. To be seen even talking with you could surely ruin mine." She held her head high.

"This is not the end of the matter, Kate."

"Oh, sir." She smiled up to him sweetly. "This is the very end for us. I have long wished to discomfit you in the way you have many times discomfited me. I think perhaps I have succeeded? If you could only see your face." She laughed as she turned her attention to the podium where the musicians were finally settling down.

Alexander was livid but knew better than to put himself on public display, and remained quiet for some moments. But as the first ensemble began, he turned to Kate. "You are a damnable woman!"

"Yes, I suppose I am," Kate shrugged her shoulders, but no smile passed her lips. "But I'm twenty-seven years now and can no longer afford to play at being a Bath miss. I must have a care for myself, don't you agree? No, I can see that you don't, but it makes no difference. You don't have to. It's nothing to me."

"And I'm nothing to you?" Alexander demanded, shocked by her cold-heartedness.

"No. Should you be?" Kate asked sincerely.

"Then I'm expendable." He pursed his lips. "I see now how you could let me play the fool that day."

"Oh, yes, it was quite easy," she lied sadly. The evening was not turning out quite as she and Emily had planned, and she did not fully understand why, but at least the Marquess finally knew where she stood. Was there not satisfaction in that, she wondered vaguely?

The first chords of music resounded in the conservatory and all conversation came to a halt. Kate sat still for some time, pretending to hear the music and not daring to move, but so terribly aware of the angry young man sitting beside her. She felt the brush of his coat as he folded his arms across his chest only to uncross them restlessly.

The very air around them reverberated with his rage and she knew she had pushed him quite far.

The concert seemed interminable but the hour was soon up and everyone rose to applaud. Kate knew not where to look and was grateful to hear Lord Edward's solid voice from behind. "Halo, Kate, watch your step. Dancing and dinner this way. So-so music, didn't you think?"

Kate followed his path, murmuring various things that he didn't even hear. "Do you join us for supper, Alex?" she heard him address the Marquess. But what he said she knew not and he was gone when she finally found the courage to face him.

"Got a buzz in his head," Lord Edward mumbled as his friend disappeared. "Well, it's just you and I, Kate, and I for one am for the lobster patties," and they made their way along with the crowd to the ballroom where a cold collation had been set up.

Unable to eat, Lord Alexander had instead taken himself into the card room, downing four brandies along the way. He pretended to play a few hands of faro but his thoughts strayed unavoidably. Unable to concentrate, he returned to roam the ballroom, and as he watched Kate dance by with partner after partner, jealous rage tore at him. Damnation, she wouldn't get away with this night's work, and as the orchestra struck up a waltz he found his way to her side. Before she could stop him, Lord Alexander drew Kate roughly into his

164

arms, a forbidding light in his eyes. "Ours," he commanded quietly.

"Let me go," she whispered fiercely, but the Marquess held her firmly in his grip as he spun her onto the dance floor.

"You're besotted," Kate pleaded, but he made no reply. "I'll faint, I swear it," she threatened, but he only tightened his hold as they reeled among the other dancers, fairly flying. She could only cling to him tightly as they went round at a dizzying pace, until he finally maneuvered them through a door and out to the terrace. He thrust her onto a stone bench where she gasped for air as he watched her through cold gray eyes.

"Please," she cried distractedly, "what would you have of me?" But he only continued to stare silently as she trembled. Then suddenly she felt herself lifted and carried into his embrace. She stiffened, ready to resist, and fleetingly wondered whether she was resisting his importunities or her own impulses. In the end, it did not matter.

"My, my, what a pretty picture they make. Don't you agree, Sally dear?" The startled couple looked up to see Maria Sefton and her friend, the notorious Lady Jersey, standing portentously by the door.

"I . . . I beg your ladyships, do . . . do not . . . misunderstand," Kate stammered, mortified beyond further speech.

"We don't misunderstand, dear Kate. We have perfectly good vision." Lady Sefton laughed softly, although furious at having apparently lost the Marquess to Kate Barrister.

"What an *on dit*," smiled Lady Jersey, who loved a breath of scandal while keeping her own affairs eminently discreet.

"I beg you will keep this private," Lord Alexander grinned as he kept his hold of Kate.

"This story speaks for itself," exclaimed Lady Sefton irritably. "Miss Barrister found in the arms of the elusive Marquess. And I thought this party was going to be a bore. Well, Kate, your secret is out, but never fear, perhaps your staunch reputation will stand you in good stead."

Lord Alexander intervened sternly. "I beg you will not be thinking to alarm this lady with the spread of malicious lies on the morrow. I should take it personally were she to be discomposed by anything untoward which reached her ears."

"You would take it personally?" gasped Lady Sefton. "That would certainly be a first. Are we to assume, then, that you are not molesting Kate?"

"I was obviously not molesting her," Lord Alexander returned coldly, as he watched the conversation take its predictable turn.

"Then it is agreed," Lady Sefton sneered, "that the lady was reciprocating. But I cannot countenance such goings-on here. Your affair may be conducted privately, but . . ."

"Affair?" Kate echoed faintly.

"I beg your pardon, ladies, you don't seem to have heard. But then, it hasn't been publicly announced," Lord Alexander said cryptically.

"Heard what? Announced what?" The suspicious women pounced on his words.

"Of our engagement, *bien entendu*," said the future Duke of Landonshire coolly, but smiling grandly to himself. There would be the devil to pay for that one!

"Engagement? Betrothal?" gushed Lady Jersey archly, although ably feigning contrition. "Kate, forgive me. I thought . . . but never mind. Come here and let me kiss you. A handsomer couple I could not find," and she nudged Lady Sefton decisively.

"Congratulations, Kate," that woman was forced to offer. "This certainly is unexpected. I'd never have guessed, from your earlier behavior. I shall spread the glad tidings this very night; and look forward to reading the announcement in *The Gazette*," she added tartly. She took Lady Jersey's arm to depart and could not resist a backward glance, as if to catch them in a lie—but Kate and Lord Alexander stood still until they were gone.

"Let that be a lesson to you on the perils of flirtation," Lord Alexander finally spoke, a distinct note of sarcasm in his voice.

"Flirting? I?" Kate cried. "More a lesson on the perils of drink, I make no doubt."

"And very fine brandy it was too," he smiled wickedly.

"Engaged?" she whispered, ignoring his outburst, panic beginning to rise. "Engaged," she repeated, disbelieving.

"Tut, madame. That's the least of your prob-

167

lems. This engagement can be broken on the morrow. In fact, I place the matter entirely in your hands. The explanation of its brevity I leave to you. I shall agree to any story you put forth."

"But it was you who made that idiotic announcement," she snapped, distraught.

"Ungrateful wench. Had I much time in which to consider alternatives? You, on the other hand, have until daybreak to do so. That's more than sufficient, don't you think?"

"No, I don't. I can't imagine what I'm going to say," she stamped her foot impatiently. "Oh, did you have to invent such an awful explanation?"

"My condolences," snorted Lord Alexander. "If the idea of being engaged to me so repulses you, I can think of half a dozen women who would beg to trade places," at which Kate gasped. "You must excuse my bravado," he continued, "but it springs from a long suppressed desire to shake you. I can only add that the thought of being married to you fills me with no less repugnance. On that, I bid you good evening," and he turned furiously about and was gone. And for the second time in Kate's life, Lord Alexander walked away, when he should have stayed.

Thirteen

As to the breaking of their engagement, it must be stated at the outset that neither party ever stood the slightest chance of doing so.

The morning after the ridotto, Kate was awakened by her maid bearing the cards of Lady Jersey and Lady Sefton. She was told that both women had settled themselves comfortably in the breakfast parlor, determined not to leave until they had words with the mistress. Kate rose quickly and frantically began to strive for some story with which to explain away the previous evening's episode for she had no illusion as to their reason for calling so early.

By the time she had finished her ablutions, Lady Brougham arrived, and a second pot of chocolate served. Three dejected suitors soon followed, vociferously protesting her engagement, and still she had not conjured up any sane story which would disabuse them of the notion that she was betrothed to the Marquess. She shrugged her shoulders and descended. They were upon her, en masse, when she entered the parlor, and it did later seem to her the whole of the haute ton was also, that day.

By three that afternoon the tea urn had been replenished four times and cook was in the throes of baking pastry in preparation for the evening's threatened onslaught of well-wishers. The servants, having heard the news, themselves caught the holiday spirit and there was no doubt they were pleased with their mistress's brilliant alliance. Knowing what snobs her servants could be, Kate would have been greatly amused, had she not been so distressed.

The news spread so overwhelmingly fast, and so thoroughly, that Kate never had a moment to present the facts of the matter to anyone. People tumbled in and out all morning and afternoon, offering their congratulations, laughing, gossiping, espying friends and forming cliques, and in general, having a good time. An untold number of questions were posed and dissected on the subjects of chapels, wedding gowns, trousseaus, honeymoons, and gifts. The Prince Regent even sent a jade snuffbox along with his promise to attend her wedding personally. And although it was only delicately hinted at (he was known for his impeccable manners) Prinny also offered to be best man.

By afternoon tea Kate yet found herself affianced to Lord Alexander and a deep sense of foreboding began to set in. Her drawing room was filled with visitors when Emily was announced, and she felt a mixture of relief and embarrassment.

"Kate Barrister, how do you do it?" Emily grinned broadly and hugged her friend. Her entrance had caused some consternation, so huge was she with child, but Emily looked so rosy and complacent that everyone's fears were soon allayed.

Kate shook a finger at her friend. "Does Edward know you're here?" She drew her to an alcove that they might be private for a moment.

Emily was sheepish. "No. You know he would never let me out alone. That's why I waited until he left for the House. He's giving a speech this afternoon for the closing session and then he thinks he's taking me to Crimshaw."

"Not today?"

"No, but he means to leave within the week, possibly less." Emily looked very rebellious. "I won't go peaceably unless you promise to visit, Kate."

"Emily!" Kate frowned.

"Don't worry," she grinned, smoothing down the lamb's wool pelisse Lord Edward insisted she wear although it was late June. "And don't let's waste time; Edward might track me down. I know you can't go into detail now, Kate, but pray tell, what's going on?" Kate's eyes welled with tears and Emily pressed her hand. "I knew it wasn't going to be simple."

"It's not." Kate smiled valiantly. "It never is, with me. Lady Sefton found us in a compromising position, and to extricate us, Lord Alexander told her a corker!"

"I guess I don't have to guess."

"No, you don't. And this is the result. I was supposed to pass it off as a joke, or something. But as you can see, it's out of my hands. Emily, what will I do? What can I do, now the die is cast—no one in this room would believe me."

Emily eyed Kate's guests speculatively. "No, I think not, more's the pity. Well, this is what comes of encouraging Kate Barrister to flirt."

"Oh, Emily, I never got a chance to do any of the things we planned. The Marquess and I had a battle royal and then . . ." Kate gestured helplessly, "he got drunk and . . . and . . . tried to . . . oh, Emily, what shall I do?"

"He got drunk? He tried to . . . ?" Emily's eyes widened.

"Yes, yes, it was awful," Kate wailed.

"Awful? Mmm, how interesting," and she began to think very hard.

"And by the by, he knew all the time that I was not married," Kate threw out to complete the sad saga. "I don't know how, but he did. Perhaps he got it from Lady Sefton. He addressed me as 'Miss Barrister' the moment we met. Oh, he was dreadfully mean, quite insulting really, but dear Edward came to my rescue."

Emily eyed her curiously, her busy brain pondering a different aspect of the story: "But why did he try to . . . ?"

Kate turned pink and wished she had left that

part out. "I told you—he was besotted! He admitted it. 'Brandy' he said, 'and very good stuff too,' he said . . . ooh, he is an impossible man." And at that precise moment the "impossible man" was announced. "Oh, Emily he will never understand why the hoax has continued, and at what startling pace." But Kate need never have worried. It was a full twenty minutes before Lord Alexander was able to make his way to her side, doing so amidst much laughter, a tinkling of applause, and also enduring many handclasps.

"Kate," he smiled tenderly as he took hold of her hands, his play-acting very impressive to her. "Emily," he nodded, as that young woman diplomatically excused herself (to secure a nearby seat convenient for observation). Emily thought the Marquess did not look to be as nearly upset as one might expect, given the true facts.

"My lord," Kate said shyly, "it is kind of you to call. Now you can see for yourself the quandary I am in, for I feared you would never believe me. Half London has been here today, congratulating me on my betrothal and already the gifts flow in. The news of our engagement has spread like wildfire and I've been too cowardly to put out the flame," she explained in an agitated fashion.

"Don't apologize until you've heard my news," he replied, strangely unperturbed. "I was awakened this morning with a shower of champagne, while still abed I am sorry to say. Some of my 'dearest' friends deemed that the only fitting way to congratulate the most eligible bachelor in London for having got himself leg-shackled. They were drunk as lords, if you will pardon the expression," but she couldn't see that he was so unamused. "I have been dragged through half the pubs in London by seven besotted fools who paid not the least heed to my protestations."

"I can readily sympathize," Kate said quickly, "the question is, what to do? Perhaps it's best if one of us leaves London, temporarily, of course."

Lord Alexander smiled. "Again?"

Kate glanced up sharply. "I don't understand—" She frowned.

"Never mind. But you're wrong, my dear. There is another solution to the problem," he proposed offhandedly, intentionally avoiding her eyes. "I have been thinking . . . we could marry."

"Marry?" Kate cried in hushed tones. "Marry you merely because of a bad joke, my lord? Spare me such chivalry. The idea is ridiculous and betrays an unwarranted lack of sensibility."

"There are worse things in this world, my girl," Lord Alexander said sternly, "scandal is one of them. Do I understand correctly that the Prince has acknowledged our betrothal?"

"Yes," she answered hesitantly, "but that is no matter. We can let things die down awhile, then perhaps, in September, we can announce an amicable separation."

"That's all very well, but what shall we do until then?" he asked, feeling disappointed, for the day's turn of events had not displeased him nearly as much as he pretended.

"Disappear, as I have suggested," Kate returned, exasperated.

"But that will cause comment. In any case, it does not speak to the immediate problem, by which I mean tonight, tomorrow, and the days following. How do you want me to treat you, given our circumstance?" and this time his eyes fastened on hers.

"Oh, I don't know," cried Kate, thoroughly confused and fast perceiving a headache. "I must go and lie down, think things out."

"All right, then," he whispered, "I shall attend you this evening. But stay a moment and calm yourself. I don't wish a public scene by my bride." He bent to kiss her lightly. Kate's hands flew to her cheek in acute embarrassment, and for the first time in two years, Lord Alexander threw back his head in genuine laughter. Eyes turned in their direction; guests nodded knowingly. "Only playing my part, love." The Marquess smiled but his eyes held a curious light.

Words failed Kate, but it was no matter, for he was gone in an instant. How ironic, she thought. She would have married him that very day, if only once he had told her he loved her. But he had made it clear that he was only pretending affection for propriety's sake.

That fact was not so very clear to Emily who had observed all from afar. Indeed, she had been given much food for thought, none of which she sought to share with Kate: her friend was obviously in no manner approachable. Indeed, Kate had disappeared, so Emily took herself home to do some honest and quiet thinking.

Kate was in the midst of packing next day when Lord Alexander barged his way into her boudoir. "My lord," she gasped.

"Damnation, Kate, stop 'lording' me or I shall begin to call you 'Marchioness!' " Surveying the disorganized room he then demanded to know just where she thought she was going.

"To Ramdomm," Kate flashed, "did you think I would stay?"

"You will, if I have anything to say to the matter. Which I do," he proclaimed inexorably. Another hour and he would have missed her, he realized in vexation. She would bear close watching in future.

"I won't stay another day. I've thought it over and really, it's the only solution. Yesterday was only a small taste of what will surely continue if we remain engaged. I couldn't bear it, really I couldn't." Kate's eyes filled with tears as she resumed packing her trunks.

"One coward in the family is enough, my girl," Alexander decreed cryptically. "You will stay and we'll work this out together. I'll countenance no scandal attributed to my name. It may interest you to know that Prinny expects us to meet him at Hyde Park at eleven and he's bringing Lady Hertford. He wishes to make the acquaintance of my future Duchess, and you won't fail him, 'pon my word."

"But that's as good as an announcement in *The Gazette*," Kate paled.

"Perhaps." Alexander smiled gently, not wishing to press the point. "But it hasn't come to that, quite."

At this news, Kate sank into the nearest chair. The situation became more complicated every hour. She glanced helplessly up at Alexander but his face betrayed no empathy. She could not possibly know that only fierce pride prevented his rushing to her side and betraying all his passion.

The truth of the matter was that Alexander had not slept at all the previous night. He had paced his sitting room until his valet swore the carpeting would be ruined, and he had polished off an entire bottle of Napolean. It had given him a tremendous hangover, which accounted for his present irritability, but it had not shaken his determination. Fate had seemed to deal him a deadly blow at Lady Sefton's ridotto, and the events following had seemed even more disastrous. Yet it had come to him, halfway through his bottle of brandy, that given a bit of luck and a good deal of subtlety, he might reverse the tide of events in his favor. He loved Kate desperately, he quite knew that now, and had hoped that one day she might come to love him. But he was honest enough to admit that on that last point he hadn't any qualms: he would marry Kate Barrister before the year was out, or he would know the reason why.

So it was that Alexander, with a bit of that

looked-for luck, was able to prevent Kate's leaving London, and to persuade her instead to meet the Prince of Wales. And if the truth be known, it was Alexander who had contrived this very public meeting and not the Prince, as he had implied. (It went without saying that Prinny was not above a little duplicity when it came to helping his friends, especially in matters of the opposite sex. And Alexander had become a great favorite since his return, and ever since the Prince had begun to feud with Brummell.) This was the first of many threads of an invisible, but inviolable, web he planned to spin around his beloved. The general idea was to enmesh Kate so deeply into the fabric of their engagement as to make it impossible for her to cry off without causing an uproar. Fortune indeed smiled on his lordship, for when they returned from their royal outing they found a letter from Eustace.

"My word," Kate explained, holding the letter aloft in one hand, while she untied her satin bonnet ribbons with the other. "Whatever next, I can't imagine."

"What's amiss?" said Alexander, about to take his leave.

"Aunt Eustace and your father are coming to London Tuesday. It seems the Duke has unexpected business to attend to and she has decided to accompany him. She wishes to do a bit of shopping, she writes, and wants to know if I can return to Landonshire with them, it's so close to the end of the season."

"Well, that's your decision, of course. Summer is upon us," he commented briefly, not wishing to overplay his hand.

"They can have no idea as to what they're walking into. They won't have heard of our engagement yet, and I can't imagine what a shock it will be for them," she frowned.

Alexander smiled to himself, but outwardly his face was unperturbed. "Then it is to be hoped that you will break it to them gently."

"I shall have to tell them the truth, sir. They will be even more horrified, I assure you. I shall sink below reproach. Oh, what a horrible mess," she sighed, pressing a hand to her eyes.

I can't think of anything more marvelous, thought Alexander roguishly, except for that last, which I shall put to mend. "Why tell them the truth?" he asked aloud. "You shall only succeed in embarrassing them unnecessarily, and that will make all of us uncomfortable. Leave them to think what they will, and when we break our engagement, at least the truth will have been kept to ourselves. Any other course of action would cause great pain, don't you agree?" He held his breath.

Kate was silent, then turned to stare coolly up at him. "You seem to be taking this entire matter awfully calmly, I think. As the man who so ably represented his complete distaste for this situation, you are exceedingly cooperative, of late. What is the advantage to you?"

Seeing Kate looking so beautiful as she stood

bathed in the golden light of afternoon, Alexander was hard put to answer. Since he had determined to marry her, his patience knew no bounds, but he had learned his past lessons well and was keeping himself in check. This was his last chance, well he knew, to capture this woman for his own, and he would cut off his arm before he said a wrong word or made a wrong move.

"I have already told you," he answered lightly, "I will have no breath of scandal coupled with my name."

"Pah! You've a reputation these many years as a libertine and rake, what matter now?" she asked suspiciously.

It was all he could do not to laugh, but he put his sternest face forward. "My reputation, as you have so delicately put it, has, if nothing else, always been restricted to certain boundaries generally acceptable to society. Nobody minds a libertine when he confines himself to the demimonde. You, on the other hand, are an excessively respectable woman. The very fact that society did not ostracize you when you set up your own establishment bears out my argument."

"Pray don't gammon me, my lord," Kate returned caustically.

"Oh, I'm not," he smiled. "It's your reputation which would ruin me, if it were found out that I had hoaxed such an innocent as you. I would never be accepted into any respectable household again, and I must needs look to the future. One day I must marry and have children and they will eventually want entrée into society. I mustn't spoil their possibilities, you understand." Well, that was doing it a bit brown, he thought ruefully, but supposed it would have to do.

"I see," said Kate thinly. "You are a cold-hearted man, Lord Alexander, but not without foresight. Much luck I wish your children, and heaven only help your wife."

"Heaven help me," corrected Alexander ambiguously, and quickly made his adieu before Kate could follow that up.

Fourteen

The Duke and Duchess of Landonshire arrived in London three days later, amidst an early summer storm. A messenger brought word of their safe arrival to Kate only moments after she had received Lord Alexander who insisted upon accompanying her to Berkeley Square. He claimed it only fitting that the news of their engagement be broken by them together, before word of it arrived through the grapevine.

The Duke and Duchess were enjoying high tea after their long journey when the young couple arrived. Eustace was agape when they were jointly announced, but wisely held her tongue and used her powers of observation instead. The Duke, always solicitous, made them all comfortable and rang for a fresh pot of tea.

"What a coincidence," he began after they were settled down, "your arriving here together. A pleasure to see you both on such good terms," he remarked and Kate eyed him suspiciously, but was unable to divine anything untoward.

"Not such a great coincidence, sir," returned

Lord Alexander wryly. "We're not quite sure of our relationship, given your marriage, but we have been seeing something of each other, of late. I do hope you won't be shocked."

"Shocked?" repeated the Duke, "why on earth should we be shocked? We're family now, and it does you justice to have a care for Kate's well-being. Not that the little miss will appreciate my saying so, I dare say," he added with a twinkle, having seen Kate's brow go up.

"Well, I certainly appreciate it," interjected Eustace, "for I own I cannot feel that comfortable thinking of Kate living alone here in London. I never did. A woman alone is prey to all sort of . . ." but she broke off, sensing her niece's consternation. "I know it's what you wanted, my dear," she added, pressing Kate's hand, "and you have had your way. Not a breath of scandal have I heard since you set up on your own, nor did I expect to. Your behavior has been exemplary, as I thought it would be, but I worry all the same."

"Aunt . . . your grace," Kate attempted in a faltering voice.

"Please, my dear," said the Duke, bending to give her a peck on the cheek, "don't be impatient with our concern for you. We only want the best for our 'daughter,' which is how we think of you."

"You're very kind, Duke, and I'm very undeserving," she whispered humbly.

"Kate, how can you ever say such a thing? Why you've been nothing less than a daughter to us," Eustace asserted indignantly.

"Oh, Aunt," smiled Kate tightly, "it's only that I have news which may come as a shock and I hope you won't be too upset with my having given you no warning. It was all so sudden," she finished lamely and looked to Lord Alexander for support.

"What my darling is trying to tell you," he took up, refusing to spare her blushes, "is that she has graciously consented to become my wife." The room was instantly still.

"Goodness me," cried the Duke, collecting his wits, "when did all this happen?"

Kate could hardly respond, so put out of countenance was she, so Lord Alexander filled the breach. "Some time ago, Father, but we wanted to be sure, and have been keeping it under wraps. Unfortunately, this is no longer the case. The whole of London found out days ago and you must prepare yourself for the onslaught of congratulators who will soon be upon you in droves, if our experience is any example. I'd notify the cook immediately, if I were you," he jested to lighten Kate's mood, but saw it was to little avail.

"I shall try to sustain myself." Eustace smiled as she came back to life. "What a handsome couple you are, to be sure. I shall be necksore from preening like a peacock at the match you have made. Oh my darling children, I'm so happy for you."

Kate bent her head in mortification and Lord Alexander quickly came to sit beside her. Putting his arm about her shoulders, he looked to his parents. "Don't mind Kate, she's become sentimental of late. Happiness does strange things to a woman, don't you agree, Stepmama?" Eustace did not agree, but did not say so. She had never known Kate to be sentimental in her life, but decided to let the matter pass, momentarily.

"A love match," the Duke smiled, bending to kiss his new daughter. "I couldn't be more pleased, although I don't understand how my errant son could capture such a prize."

"I consider myself the most fortunate of men, Father, and have sworn to be the best of husbands. But Kate only knows a few of my bad points," he grinned, "and I don't wish her enlightened further or she'll throw me over before I've had a chance to reform. Or be reformed," he added with a comical sigh.

"Lord Alexander," Kate started, and felt the Marquess's fingers dig imperceptibly into her shoulder. "Alexander," she revised, "if you find the idea of reformation so overwhelming perhaps we ..." but Lord Alexander stopped her next words with a quick kiss.

"I'm sorry, my love, but I couldn't help myself, lest you doubted the sincerity of my affections." She could not tell if he smiled behind his beard, but his eyes were certainly somber. She swore to herself he would regret this day's business, but the Duke interrupted her thoughts.

"I for one am delighted to witness my son's affectionate manner for it portends a happy marriage. I pray you will both be as happy as we, and I joyously bestow my blessings."

"How soon did you plan to wed?" inquired Eustace matter-of-factly.

"Next June, we thought," answered her niece uneasily.

"Next June?" exclaimed Eustace. "Well, of course that's up to you, but that's an awfully long time, don't you think?" At which point Lord Alexander decided things were going swimmingly.

"Not at all," Kate demurred, giving her affianced a speaking glance, but that gentleman remained stoically silent.

"I should have thought two young lovers such as you would be anxious to exchange vows as quickly as possible!"

"Oh yes," Lord Alexander agreed politicly, then let his innocent stepmama carry on.

"Well, then. There's no reason to delay."

"But weddings take forever to plan," Kate protested. "I need a trousseau and gown, to begin with. And invitations must be sent, the banns posted, dinners planned. The list is endless."

"Nonsense," fluttered her ladyship, "such details take care of themselves." She raised a brow and grew serious. "You do want to marry his lordship, don't you?" and a hushed silence filled the room. Kate's eyes filled with tears and she went to kneel beside her aunt. "Of course I do, dearest Aunt. I just didn't think to rush the matter considering I have a lifetime to ... to spend ... with ..."

"There, there, my dear. I didn't mean to doubt you. I just don't like to see you spend another lonely winter at Randomm. You must do as you think best, of course."

"One might think of me," smiled Lord Alexander, absently toying with his whiskers.

Eustace turned to stare coolly at her stepson and the Duke hastily intervened. "I would imagine that my son also does not look forward to a long and unnecessary wait, but he certainly does not present the matter delicately," he tacitly admonished his offspring.

"Well, I don't think that the height of delicacy either," returned Alexander sardonically, but privately appreciated the turn of the conversation.

"Well, Kate," asked the Duke, "what do you think? Winters can be very long, and if it's only the prenuptial arrangements which daunt you, well, I can certainly promise you this: you could be married in autumn, two months from now, in such style as to be the most envied bride of the decade. But, of course, it's your decision. And Alex's, I dare say."

Alexander could feel the not-so-subtle pressure put upon Kate but would not interfere, having his own interests at heart. No doubt he would catch the sharp edge of her tongue when next they were private, but her commitment seemed worth the risk. He would tell her his hand had been forced. "Well, if Kate is agreeable . . . but then, I'm completely at her mercy," he said to no one, a shade too seriously.

"You are too kind," murmured Kate, her green eyes barely concealing her wrath. Then she rose abruptly and turned to Eustace. "I have a dresser's appointment and must leave immediately. You know how Madame Shields can be." Then, to her betrothed: "Do you stay and make any arrangements you wish. I leave the matter entirely in your capable hands," and she had to smile at his evident surprise. They tried to detain her but Kate could no longer trust herself not to be hysterical and tumble forth with the truth. She craved fresh air with which to calm herself, and think, and made good her escape.

Home she sped, where she threw herself heavily onto a sofa, and from which she rose just as abruptly. She had plenty to think about and thought to seek out Emily, but no, that poor girl had enough problems and Kate refused to burden her further. In the final analysis, she could only hope to ride out the engagement without further difficulty. After all, she had known it would not be easy. But her conscience worried her—she hated hoaxing the Duke and Duchess, and quite lost a night's sleep over the matter.

Three days later the Duke and Duchess were pleased to hold forth at a ball in honor of the betrothal. The ball only made official what had already taken the ton by storm a few days previous; nonetheless, invitations were at a premium, only a select three hundred having been invited. Hyde Park was bereft of a great many of its patrons those days preceding the ball, so many of the quality needing to devote additional time to their dressmakers and seamstresses. Husbands groaned audibly at the bills that piled high, but their wives simply ignored their protests, intent only on dressing to the nines for what promised to be "the" sociality of the season.

The only woman who spent her time quietly, in all of London, was she who was to be honored. Eustace, knowing that Kate was incapable of handling such large-scale arrangements, had taken immediate charge of preparations with Kate's grateful consent. The Duke had tactfully withdrawn so as not to distract his wife at her work, more than grateful to exchange the constant hubbub lately found in his home for the relative peace of White's. Alexander, on the other hand, was not to be found anywhere, having discreetly taken himself off to Brighton for a few days: he did not want Kate to flare up at him, and possibly back down, which she seemed inclined to do when he was about. Finally, Kate had bid good-bye to her truest friend after Emily's husband insisted she was too close to birthing to remain any longer in London. After a closed session together (wherein Emily prayed she had given Kate enough moral sustenance to see her through the ball) the young women shared a tearful departure until Lord Edward could stand it no longer.

"My word," he exclaimed, vastly annoyed at the length his horses were made to wait, "why don't you just come down to visit us, Kate, after the ball's over? We'd obviously love to have you, and

Alex, too. Emily's not all that ready to . . . to . . . you know."

Kate smiled through her tears. "Maybe. I'll see. It depends on . . . oh, Emily, I'll try to be strong and do you proud."

"And so you shall, Kate," Emily cried, "and then come down to Crimshaw. It's a lovely estate, and not all that far, and then I can hear all the details in person."

"I'll try," Kate promised weakly.

"Dash it all, Kate," Lord Edward grumbled, "I never saw such a one for complicating a man's life. Alex should have married you when he returned, like I told him! Wouldn't have to make such a big fuss now."

"Married me when he returned?" Kate repeated dumbly. "What on earth are you talking about?"

"Don't I speak the King's English?" Sir Edward sighed visibly. "He visited me a day or so after he paid you some dreadful morning call. Said you were rude to him and all. Quite put me out of countenance, Kate, I do assure you."

"But why?" Emily patiently drew him out.

"Because, dearest love, I had it in my foolish head that they would make a charming couple. Said so, too."

"But that means . . ." Emily's eyes widened, but Kate finished for her.

"It means that he knew I wasn't married long-before Maria Sefton's ridotto! Oh, how he must have laughed as he led me on, play-acting his indignation!"

Emily placed a soothing hand on her friend's arm. "Kate, you've a dangerous look in your eyes." Kate took Emily's hands in her own.

"Don't be a quiz, Emily, I've nothing in my head. But it makes everything so much more interesting, don't you agree?"

"Well . . ." Emily hesitated, taking note of the new tone of Kate's voice.

"Dash it all, what's going on?" Lord Edward exclaimed. "You women always make the most of everything, even when it doesn't exist. Between the two of you something's been hatched, and it smells a bad egg."

Emily climbed awkwardly into the carriage and bid her husband do the same. "Never mind, I'll tell you later. Oh, Kate, do be careful. He can be so very devious, I see now. Have a care, my little innocent. And come down to Crimshaw when it's over. Promise me?"

"You may depend on it," Kate smiled bravely up to her friend. "And do you have a care, dear Emily," and with that the carriage took off.

So it was that Kate was quite alone in the days before the ball, but quite contrary to Lord Alexander's forebodings, having no thoughts of running away. Nonetheless, she had been struck by Lord Edward's parting information and was at odds how to deal with this information. In a strange way, she felt "armed" possessing information Lord Alexander did not know she had; in some way it must have its use. But having no one to confide in, she felt at a loss how to bring things about to her advantage, although she was hardly aware what she meant by that—she was only clear about having felt ill-used.

By the time Kate descended the night of the ball, she still had no idea how to utilize her knowledge of Lord Alexander's perfidy. What she did know, when he arrived to escort her to Berkeley Square, was that she felt singularly composed. It was this strength which enabled her to glance coyly from beneath her lashes at the elegant and handsome man whom she had heretofore found intimidating.

"How good of you to come so promptly," she smiled deceptively. "Will I do as the happily affianced, do you think?" and with no small trace of amusement she did an outrageous pirouette. Dressed in shimmering silk of the purest cream, the bodice trimmed low off the shoulders with satin rouleaux, she could not help but be aware of her impact. Her hair had been worked in the simplest fashion to set off an emerald tiara, and emeralds lay lightly on her neck.

Lord Alexander smiled and gently took her hand to bestow a kiss. "Admirably, Kate, well you know. But I don't begrudge you the compliment." Then carefully, "I could not have chosen a lovelier wife, had I the opportunity or time."

Kate frowned. "Is it your intent, sir, to dampen my spirits so early in the night?"

"No, Kate, you mistake my meaning," he hastened to amend, "I only meant . . ."

"Never mind." Kate waved his apology aside

with an airy gesture and permitted a small smile. "I understand my position quite well and in two months' time," she shrugged lightly, "it will be of no moment. But tonight—well, tonight I shall abandon my folly on the dance floor until, hopefully, someone saves me from my recklessness." Good lord, did she say that? Kate fought to suppress her laughter and warned herself to slow down for Lord Alexander was eyeing her with some curiosity.

"If mademoiselle would permit me to champion her?" Alexander tried to match her mood, and this time Kate did laugh, to his confusion.

"Foolish man. I would suppose it must be you if we are 'engaged'! Do you forget so soon we'll really have the gossips talking." And she quit the room with a flourish, leaving a rather dazzled Marquess to follow.

The drive to Berkeley Square was accomplished in twenty minutes during which the couple occupied themselves with small talk. Alexander drank in the barely discernible profile of his betrothed, and found it no small feat now to contain his impulse to catch her in his arms. At the same time that his hands itched to move, his head told him Kate would deliver a resounding slap to any overture he might make. Schooling himself to bide his time, he pulled a small package from his greatcoat.

"It would not do for you to appear bereft of this." He placed the box in her gloved fingers.

"My lord?" Kate turned up a puzzled face.

"I knew you'd not think of such a thing. It was my grandmother's ring, and now it is yours. Temporarily," he added, in concession to her strange mood.

"I can't . . ." Kate faltered, eyes misty.

"You must. People will talk. Please don't start to cry. You'll turn puffy if you do. Now, do put it on," he insisted huskily and opened the box as she removed her glove. It was an enormous diamond in a marquise setting made heavier by surrounding emeralds.

"You may have it reset, if you like, but it must do for tonight."

"Thank you for remembering," Kate whispered, sincerely touched.

"Then shall I have a kiss on it, Kate?" he murmured, his eyes glinting mysteriously.

"What?" She turned away in no small confusion then turned awkwardly back to brush the lips he boldly presented her.

He felt his hands move, and laughed silently to himself. Have a care, old man, go gently. Then the carriage was halted and a footman appeared to usher them on into the evening.

The Duchess had really outdone herself, everyone agreed. The mansion sparkled with lights from every room, each chandelier and candle branch burnished to reflect their light. Stephanotis had been entwined about the entire banister leading up to the main ballroom, silver ribbons falling gracefully from its fragile branches. A buffet table took the entire length of the room and had been laden with every delicacy imaginable. Indeed, all was of a ducal splendor. Somewhat overwhelmed as she mounted the stairs, Kate felt the Marquess's arm go protectively about her waist and was almost grateful for its presence. Remembering Emily's advice on the gentle art of persuasion, she decided to say nothing, and was rewarded by the glimmer in his eye, and was further astonished when he bent to kiss her lightly. Perhaps there was something to Emily's advice, after all, but suddenly remembering the circumstances of their betrothal, she checked her sense of well-being.

The Duke and Duchess greeted them effusively and bade them join the receiving line. It was a full hour before they could quit their greetings and feel free to wander among the guests. Prinny, who had arrived at an hour considerably early for him, insisted on claiming the bride-to-be's first waltz. *"Le droit de seigneur,"* he teased Kate as he led her to the floor. Given his penchant for beautiful women, it was not surprising when he claimed a second dance. When it was over, Alexander tactfully drew his fiancée aside.

"I've something to show you," he whispered, ushering her into an adjacent room and was amused by the startled look in her eyes. "Gifts," he grinned, "from all over Europe. It gives one pause to think."

"It certainly does," Kate exclaimed in an awe-stricken tone, a worried look coming over her face. "Oh, Lord Alexander, I mean Alexander, what shall we do? We are perpetrating a fraud."

"Not at all," he smiled, "we're engaged, you know. It's our due, in the eyes of society."

"It's not our due, well you know," Kate frowned. "We must return each and every one."

"Not just now, dearest. Our engagement isn't broken yet!" Then suddenly, quite seriously, "Perhaps it will never be, if you can be persuaded . . ."

Kate paled at the import of his words and drew herself up proudly. "What are you saying, Lord Alexander? It will not do to jest at such a moment."

"I don't jest, Kate." His hands caressed her bare shoulders. "I . . ." but his next words were lost as the doors flew open to admit the Duke and Duchess.

The Duchess smiled to see new evidence of a love match for Kate. "Everyone is asking for you both, so won't you defer your lovemaking?" She was even more pleased to see her handsome stepson blush behind his beard: so, it was a love match all around! She had not been so sure, but this certainly put to rest her worries.

The Duke proudly claimed a waltz from Kate and the two couples went out to mingle once again. But Kate was distracted by Lord Alexander's words and it was all she could do to heed her steps. What had he meant? Did he really want to marry her or was all for convenience sake? He needed an heir, that she knew, and she was certainly healthy enough, if that was his purpose. Oh, Kate, don't be so cynical, she silently chided herself: he could have chosen a bride any number of times, but he chose you! He did not choose you, her baser self remonstrated: it was an accident, a fluke! Ah, but he's come so far when there really was no need, her better half maintained. And besides, there was that look he had about him— quite a few times this past hour, if the truth be known. True, agreed her baser self, content to consider this point.

Unfortunately, Kate's eyes fell on her betrothed just as he was about to lead the flirtatious Lady Marguerite Valentois into a waltz that was starting up. His head was bent intimately to take in Marguerite's whispers and Kate's baser self won out: well, he never did tell you that he loved you!

Therein lay the problem and woe to Lord Alexander, for if only he had, it would have shortened his problems considerably.

Fifteen

The next morning Kate rose to a thunderstorm which exactly reflected her mood, and on what should have been one of the happiest days of her life, she was taken by a fit of the dismals. Lord Alexander didn't love her but only toyed with her, she was sure of that now. After watching him flirt with Marguerite in the middle of his own betrothal ball, she was convinced of his insincerity: she was only a vassal whose purpose was to give him heirs, chosen as a result of circumstances. It was expedient (from his point of view, she was convinced) to continue their charade to the altar: it saved him the embarrassment of a broken engagement and the ensuing gossip that would entail. It was apparent he had no intention of changing his "womanizing" ways, and as his wife she would find this untenable.

Kate rang for Agatha and informed her they would be leaving for Crimshaw within the hour. Agatha protested loudly, but Kate would have none of it and coldly informed her she might stay or go as she pleased, but to see that Kate's portmanteau was readied. Muttering to herself on the capriciousness of the quality, Agatha flew to her tasks, loving her mistress too much to let her go alone. Kate's coachman threatened to leave her services, protesting the weather abominable for traveling, but when Kate swore to drive to Crimshaw, unescorted if need be, he shrugged his shoulders and disappeared to harness the horses, grumbling in a similar vein to that of Agatha's.

Before she left, Kate wrote a full confession to Eustace and the Duke and arranged for her footman to deliver it in the morning. She also left a note for Lord Alexander explaining that she could no longer continue their dishonorable farce. He would be very angry, she realized, but she would be gone and he'd be able to do nothing about it. Lord Alexander was horrid and if she never saw him again, well, it would just be too soon. He had behaved churlishly and she ridiculed herself for any tendre she might have harbored for him. Dispirited, she was soon hurrying her coachman on, ignoring his complaints about the rain. The downpour suited her mood, and in any case, she wouldn't be put off at this point.

Lord Alexander also bemoaned the rain as he hurried to Kate's house an hour later, steeling himself for what promised to be a memorable interview. Personally, he thought the ball had gone famously, although he knew Kate to have been embarrassed by the whole affair. But she'd gone through the charade like a trouper; he was really quite proud of her stalwartness and meant to tell her so.

He was admitted to Kate's house, and it was with a fine foreboding that he allowed himself to be shown to the library instead of the drawing room, as usual. When she did not appear, but a footman did carrying a sealed envelope, he was confirmed in fearing that something was wrong. Bidding the man leave, he lifted the missive to confirm the handwriting as Kate's, but dared not open it. She was gone, he guessed uneasily, and felt devastated. Surely it was her farewell. No doubt it would contain some not terribly prescient plea imploring him not to follow. Or think of her any further. Or contact her in any way. And somehow, given only the fact of Kate's departure, he felt he must come to some decision. He ought not allow her words, most likely written in a highly emotional state, to influence his actions.

Within minutes he rang to be shown out, and as he awaited his cape, finally read Kate's letter. He learned with surprise that her direction was Crimshaw but ignored the rest of her writing. He would follow at once, and when he found her, beg forgiveness. He would plead with her to marry him, and she would not refuse, for the thought did not bear thinking.

"Kate," Emily exclaimed, clapping her hands gleefully, "you've come as you promised! I am so glad."

"Emily, how are you? Are you well? I see you can hardly raise yourself." Kate threw off her pelisse and went to her friend's side.

"I'm fine," Emily waved Kate's concern aside, "a little cramped, but nothing more. Edward's out, but do ring for tea, the bell-rope is by the fireplace." Kate did as she was told, grateful for the suggestion, for the ride had been uncomfortably damp.

"But what are you doing here so soon, Kate? I didn't expect you until the weekend, although you know you are welcome at any time."

"Emily, I . . ."

"The party. Did it go well?" Emily interrupted, impatient for the news.

"Yes, It was lovely. Every bride's dream," Kate returned bitterly.

Emily was confirmed in suspicions. "What went wrong, Kate?"

"He . . . he . . . he . . ." Kate stammered unconsciously, and couldn't finish, giving way to a torrent of tears. Emily remembered a night so long ago when Kate had cried just so. Poor dear, how difficult it all was for her, Emily considered, as she held her friend once again. In moments, the young woman was able to contain herself.

"He spent the night flirting with every woman at the party!"

"No!" cried Emily. "He wouldn't do such a thing. You must be mistaken, you must."

"I'm not," sniffed Kate, "I saw him with my own eyes."

"With whom?"

"Marguerite Valentois, for one."

"I am amazed," said the aghast mother-to-be.

"Well you might," agreed Kate dismally, "but it's true, nonetheless. My eyesight is excellent."

Emily was silent for some moments. "I had so hoped . . . look, Kate, never mind; after all it is a fictitious engagement. Keep your chin up. Come September you can announce your separation. You may even stay here until then, if you don't mind the squalls of a newborn babe."

"You're very kind." Kate attempted a small smile. "But I wouldn't think of it. I'm heading north to Randomm, but I wanted to come down and let you know the way of things."

"Oh, Kate . . ." Emily hugged her sympathetically.

"Oh, Emily, he had been so kind, so gentle, I too had thought . . ." Kate almost broke down but steeled herself, for the sake of Emily's condition. "I will never, never trust another man!"

Just then another man entered the room. "Kate, come so soon?" Lord Edward greeted her and went to pour himself a drink. "How went the ball? A smashing success, as I've no doubt. Did you dazzle them with your ring?"

"How did you know?" Kate peered across to Lord Edward, who had drawn up a seat by the fire.

"I was there when Alex removed it from the vault. Lovely stone, awful setting. You'll want to change it, I make no doubt."

"Not really," Emily injected, hesitantly, for she and her husband had had words about Kate on their journey down. As much as Lord Edward dearly loved his friend, he found Kate no end a source of exasperation. Her complexities confused him—he was a simple man (although not insensitive) unaccustomed to shades of emotion; her difficulties with the Marquess of Landonshire were quite beyond his ken. Emily knew he would not be pleased with this latest turn of events and dreaded his reaction. She watched his bushy brows rise but was surprised by his fairly patient exclaimer: "Now what?" he turned to Kate, sardonically.

"He doesn't love me, Edward," she stated simply.

"Balderdash!" he shouted and rose to pace the room while Emily held her breath. "I spent the afternoon with him the day before Emily and I left London, the day he took his grandmother's ring to the jeweler's. Wanted it reset right then and there. Very upset when they told him it was impossible. Rang a bloody peal, he did! And at lunch he went on about whether you'd even like the stone, was in a positive dither! Quite made me ill the way he went on. I swear, Kate, if it wasn't you he was talking about, I would have left then and there! Doesn't love you? Balderdash! Balderdash, balderdash, balderdash!" He threw himself into a chair, looking very cross indeed.

Kate burst into tears while Emily was at a loss to find words to comfort them both. She turned to her husband who sat glaring at Kate. "It seems

the Marquess was not the most affectionate fi-
nancé the night of the ball."

"Balderdash!"

"Really, Edward. He spent a great deal of time
with other women. Like Marguerite Valentois.
Kate saw."

"I don't give a damn what Kate saw. She's
mistaken. He loves her, I'd stake my life 'pon it."

"Then why did he tease me so the night of Lady
Sefton's ridotto?" Kate cried.

"When did *you* never tease him? Probably
wanted to get his due! And damned right, too."
Lord Edward grumbled. "I wanted to find him
another woman to marry, but do you know, he
wouldn't hear of it? More fool him. Kate, you
could drive a man to drink," at which Kate burst
into fresh tears.

"Edward," Emily interceded, "you are being too
hard on Kate. After all, the circumstances of their
engagement are not of the most inspiring sort."

"Oh, dash it all, Emily. Alex is not the type to
go so far for so little. He has to love her."

"Has he said so?"

"Not in so many words, of course. The man isn't
built that way."

But just then Emily gave a little cry and
clenched her hands until they turned white. "It
doesn't matter now, I fear, because I think our
baby's going to make an early arrival." Her husband and friend flew to her side.

"It's my fault," cried Kate.

"Of course it is," Lord Edward barked ill-temperedly, at a loss as to how to proceed.

"Nonsense," said Emily, far more calm than they, "the pains started an hour before Kate arrived. They were more gentle but do increase, I must say." She smiled. "Edward, don't faint until you send for the doctor. Then help me to my room." She saw him disappear in search of the footman and turned to wink at Kate.

"Will he make it, do you think? Kate, it's a godsend you are here. You won't leave me, will you? I've never asked you for anything before . . . anyway, not this important. But you will see me through this, won't you?"

Kate was very upset. "Emily, how can you say such a cruel thing? I won't leave your side till you are delivered. But I must warn you." She sent her friend a worried look. "I've never engaged in this before."

Emily laughed. "Neither have I. We'll just have to be strong for each other."

An hour later, Emily's labor was quite advanced and the house quiet with anticipation. Kate had ordered sheets and towels to be boiled and plenty of hot water to be readied. True to her word, she never left her friend's side and was an enormous source of comfort. At one point, she thought she heard the doctor arrive, but minutes later, Lord Edward entered the room alone.

"How is she?" he whispered halting at the threshold and was appalled to hear his wife laugh.

"She's fine," Emily called out and bade him enter, which he did, on tenterhooks, coming to kneel beside her bed.

"A message has been left with the doctor, but our footman has returned with bad news. The doctor is in Needham visiting with another patient. Word has been sent on . . ." he faltered and Kate finished his sentence, "but you have no great hopes for his return?"

"No, but I have sent my carriage on for him, in hopes of hastening his journey. Thank the Lord you are here, Kate. Er, ah, Kate, about before. My shouting and all. I'm sorry—I meant every word I said—but I was remiss to have carried on so."

"Edward." She placed a hand on his arm. "There's no need to go on. We are friends and you can say anything you like. You spoke from your heart, I appreciate that, and know you meant well."

"Meant well?" he murmured, "that's an understatement. He's downstairs right now."

"Who?" asked Emily, vastly diverted, temporarily.

"Alex. Who else?" smiled Lord Edward. The women shot each other horrified looks. "He shall hold my hand, while Kate holds yours. He refuses to leave until it's over."

Emily cried out, a contraction was beginning, and Edward was ordered away. All thoughts of men and just about everything else were dismissed to the issue of greater things. Emily labored painfully but regularly throughout most of the night until her shrieks threatened to unman her husband, who, to Lord Alexander's amazement, refused even a single drop of brandy. The doctor never came, but a little girl did at five o'clock that morning. She was immediately named Kate Mary Louisa Brougham. Emily refused a wet nurse, wanting the pleasure for herself, and in an hour mother and babe were comfortably settled. Kate turned to seek out the new father, but not before Emily caught her arm. "Thank you, Kate," she said simply.

"Go on with you," Kate squeezed her hand. "I'll go get Edward and then you'd best sleep awhile."

It was all Kate could do to drag her feet downstairs, to enter the library where the men waited. They jumped at the sight of her.

"Is she . . . ?" Edward begged hoarsely, tears falling freely.

"They are both fine. Go and see for yourself. Emily and little Kate Mary." She laughed as he brushed past her and bounded up the stairs. Forgetting the presence of Lord Alexander she sank heavily onto a sofa and wearily closed her eyes. Lord Alexander watched, then came to kneel by her side.

"Kate," he whispered, and smiled when she made no response. She had fallen asleep from sheer exhaustion. He leaned forward to place a soft kiss on even softer lips, then lifted Kate into his arms. For all her own weight, she was a feather in his arms as he carried her up to her room.

Her eyes flickered open halfway up the stairs. "Alex," she smiled softly, weaving her arms instinctively around his neck but falling back to sleep before he met the landing. It was a decidedly content Marquess who found his way to his own room upon leaving Kate to the ministrations of Agatha.

Sixteen

The Marquess had just finished a hearty breakfast, which he had ordered served in his room so as not to disturb the Brougham household, when there was a knock at his door. Lord Edward entered at his permit to find Lord Alexander comfortably settled by the fireplace, one thumb hooked to the pocket of his waistcoat, the other hand holding a cold cigar.

"Come in," Lord Alexander grinned. "I was just going to enjoy the fruits of my reward for holding your hand last night."

Lord Edward took in his friend's easygoing demeanor and clucked to himself; his task was not going to be easy.

"How are Emily and the babe? It's so quiet I made sure they were sleeping. Have you been having another peek at your new daughter?"

"But of course," Lord Edward informed him gruffly. "They're both sleeping as if they'd not a care in the world, which they don't." Edward sent his lordship a hesitant glance. "Unlike you or I."

Lord Alexander smiled. "I was always one for rising early."

"Not as early as Kate," his host threw out coldly, annoyed at having been placed in this position.

"You don't mean to say that that poor girl is risen already? I hadn't heard a sound. Where is she? I would have words with my evil-tempered bride," he grinned, indeed anxious to do so, remembering the feel of Kate in his arms only hours before.

"She's gone," Lord Edward announced gravely and flinched as if his friend had jumped although the Marquess had not made a move.

"Explain," Lord Alexander demanded coldly, all joy gone from his eyes.

"All I know is that she arrived late yesterday afternoon terribly upset, crying and talking nonsense. We had a row, nothing big, of course, but she was being difficult. But then Kate always is," he sighed. "Emily went into labor in the middle of everything and so there was no time to straighten matters out."

"How found you out that she has left?" came Lord Alexander's icy voice. Edward was glad not to be in Kate's shoes.

"I passed her maid, Agatha, in the hall a few minutes ago. She didn't look quite right so I stopped her. The wretched woman burst into tears and babbled out the whole. Seems Kate left about an hour ago with her own coach and man. Swore her maid to secrecy—dashed fool thing to ask of a servant. The minute they are told something in secret, you are guaranteed the whole world will know—in an hour, or less! Ordered the maid to stay and play for time."

"What was her direction?"

"By the looks of it, north. To Randomm, I'll make no doubt. No sense in running away from London only to run back to it again. Nowhere else for her to go."

Alexander stared into the fire while his friend remained quiet, for all his volubility. "You are leaving something out," the Marquess prodded gently. "The nature of your disagreement."

Lord Edward turned red, blustered a bit and hedged by lighting a cigar. "Dash it all, Alex," he finally cried, "I told her she was wrong, had mistaken the looks of things. But you know Kate. A damned stubborn woman, though I love her as a sister!"

Lord Alexander's eyes were cold as they kept unspoken pressure on his friend to tell him the entire truth.

"We fought about you, as you may well guess. She came tearing down from London claiming that you had been flirting with every woman at the ball. It isn't true, Alex, is it? You wouldn't do such a thing at your own betrothal party, would you?"

"Of course not." Lord Alexander visibly paled with this revelation. "It's utter nonsense. Did she mention any names?"

"Marguerite Valentois."

"That little hussy? Surely Kate must have seen through Lady Marguerite's attempt at intimacy. I only condescended to even speak to her in order to avoid a scene. That's what Kate saw. Why didn't she simply ask me? I'd have told her the truth. Now I recall, she was so quiet on the way home, but I considered she was simply tired from the festivities. I even took especial care not to disturb her. I see I should have forced some conversation." He sadly shook his head.

"So you should have, Alex," Lord Edward gently concurred, perceiving the pain in his friend's face. "But what is more to the point is that you should have told Kate you loved her. I don't mean to obtrude," he hastened to explain, "but according to Kate, you never have."

"What?" cried Lord Alexander, coming to life, "Have I never said so?" Lord Edward could see him straining to remember, and prudently remained silent.

"Perhaps you're right, or rather Kate is. But whatever else could she think I felt? My God, I have sent her gifts, given her my grandmother's ring, been gentle and tactful and . . . and everything!"

"But you never told her you loved her, Alex. And remember, your engagement was an accident. It wasn't as if you ever courted Kate, or proposed in the normal way of things. *I* knew how seriously you took the matter but poor Kate never did. I tried to tell her last night but well, Emily . . ."

214

He shrugged his shoulder. There was nothing left to say.

A knock at the door brought a footman. Her ladyship was awake and requesting an interview with both gentlemen.

"A good idea." Lord Edward glanced up hopefully. "Emily will know how to handle Kate and give you sound advice, Alex."

Moments later they were sitting at Emily's side, her babe asleep in her arms. Alexander began to congratulate the couple but Emily cut him short.

"Lord Alexander . . . Alex," she smiled at his nod. "I will not mince words. My maid tells me Kate is gone. No doubt she has run away from you."

"So it would seem, as your husband has been explaining to me this hour last," his lordship had the grace to blush.

"Do you know why, good sir?" Emily took on a severe tone.

"It seems," he faltered, "it seems I have been remiss in explaining my feelings to Miss Barrister."

"To say the least, your lordship. With all due respect, the contrivance of your engagement was not of a nature to gladden a woman's heart, especially a woman like Kate."

"But she must have felt something," Lord Alexander floundered.

"She did, or rather, she does . . . a good deal, in fact. But that has naught to do with what she thinks you feel. At the very most," Emily carefully explained, "Kate believes that she is but the woman whom you have chosen to provide you with an heir to the duchy. She truly believes that only innate laziness prompts you to continue up to the altar."

"Laziness?" echoed the puzzled Marquess.

Emily was very patient. "You and Kate became engaged under the most inauspicious of conditions, sir! Edward and I know all, and it is our understanding that in order to avoid any scandal, you and Kate have agreed to remain betrothed until September, when you will put out that mutual differences preclude a termination of the affair. Sometime in the middle of this charade you began to act more benevolently than circumstances seemed to call for. It confused Kate, poor innocent that she is, and so untutored in the ways of love. All she could surmise was that you decided to marry her because you had nothing better to do, so to say. Hush!" Emily held up a hand to his lordship. "You were halfway to the altar. All society knew you were engaged. Why, I hear your betrothal ball was stupendous! Tell me, Marquess, is there any reason why Kate should really imagine you love her?"

The Marquess stared silently for some seconds, then, "Ah, Emily, what am I do to . . . she'll never believe the truth." He buried his head in his hands.

"What is the truth, Alex?" Emily asked gently.

"Do not you even guess?" he moaned.

"Oh, I guess. But that's not the same as being told, don't you see?"

Alexander raised his face to Emily's. "Are you not as good a friend to me also?"

"Yes, I am, dear Alex. Or at least, I am trying to be. Go now and find your lady and when you meet her . . ." she delicately left off.

Lord Alexander rose to his feet. "I want you to know one thing. Our engagement—it wasn't a hoax for my part. I thought to trick her was the only way to get her. I've loved Kate since . . . ," but Emily silenced him.

"Tell Kate. Leave it for Kate. And when the honeymoon's over, come and see us. We'll be waiting." She held out her hand, as he bent to place a gentle kiss upon it.

"You are a true lady, Viscountess Brougham. I will return during . . ."

"Christmas," interjected Lord Edward with a mischievous grin. "That *was* when it all started, wasn't it, so long ago?" He threw Lord Alexander a wink and they all laughed, confident in the future.

Twenty minutes later, Lord Alexander was packed and his horse saddled for the journey to Randomm. Before he left he met with Agatha and directed her to return to London, to pack Kate's trunks for an extended journey, and to ship them to Liverpool to await their arrival.

As he rode down the lane leading to the main thoroughfare, he took note of the day's sparkle after the night's cleansing rain. Clouds were rolling back to reveal England's blue skies and the foliage was thick with the lushness of summer. Indeed, he thought, it was a good day for a ride and he spurred his horse on to a faster trot.

Kate shivered and drew her cloak more tightly around, chilled by the early morning damp. Peering out of the coach, she was grateful to see the sun valiantly trying to penetrate the fog. It had been almost an hour since her coachman had left to make his way toward the nearest village. One of their horses had had a spill, nearly bringing them down but for old John's adroit handling of the reins. Together they had pulled the coach to the shelter of some trees, only to discover that one horse had sprained a foreleg and become totally useless. Poor John had no choice but to set out to find another, for the remaining healthy horse could not pull such a massive vehicle. Damp and cold, Kate had wished him luck and returned to the coach to await his return.

She never heard footsteps, but only saw the door swing open, and was suddenly face to face with the Marquess.

"Get out," Lord Alexander tersely ordered, incensed at finding her in this condition, having recognized her coach.

"How dare you frighten me so," Kate shuddered, trembling less from the shock of his appearance than the obvious state of his temper.

"Get out, Kate. I command you!"

"I will not!" she sniffed. "How dare you? Why

won't you leave me alone? I loathe the sight of you." She began to fumble with the opposite door in an attempt to make good her escape.

Seeing what she had in mind, and ignoring her protestations, Lord Alexander leaped into the coach, which action signaled the advent of Kate's tears. Strained by the events of the night, miserably chilled and weakened by hunger, and with no safe haven in sight, she was ripe for a shattering. Kate only vaguely recognized this as she pounded him with her fists and cursed him incoherently. Perceiving what was about, Lord Alexander clasped her firmly around although she thrashed at her imprisonment. But Kate's resources had long been spent and it was not many minutes before she lay exhausted in his arms.

"You should not have allowed John to leave you alone," Lord Alexander testily began. Kate only stared before her contemptuously and he felt his heart constrict. Lying limp in his arms, her hair in disarray, she gave the illusion of great vulnerability, but her eyes expressed none of this. He hardened himself to continue: "Anything could have happened while you were here alone. You should have waited together for a passerby to assist."

"At this hour?" Kate uttered scornfully, but he was grateful she spoke, however harshly. He would be at a loss to face her silence.

"Then you ought to have gone with John" he returned, yet knew this to be unreasonable.

Ignoring this last, Kate looked away. "Is there anything else your lordship wishes to say?"

"Yes, you wretched woman," he snapped before he could stop himself; she was so damned independent, it galled him no end. "Why did you leave London when you promised not to do so?"

"I never promised you anything, sir," said Kate with great hauteur. "I agreed to a charade that had its roots in idiocy and could plainly no longer continue. It was my wish to terminate such foolery and I was acting within my rights." She began to squirm against her confinement.

"You were quite right, of course, it could no longer continue." The Marquess ignored her attempts to escape him. "I would imagine, in retrospect, that our performance was hard on your sense of ethics, and I admit to sharing your remorse. But could you not have spoken to me first, instead of storming out of London so peremptorily?"

She stared at Lord Alexander and wondered at his sincerity. "Sir, you have never led me to believe in your constancy and I wonder that you expect me to now. I had no choice but to leave, for in my opinion, you would have drawn me into this scheme more deeply. I was . . . I was humiliated. . . ." Her voice wavered and she began to quietly weep.

"Humiliated because you thought I was flirting with Marguerite Valentois?"

"How did you . . ." Kate spluttered.

"Now who was making assumptions?" Lord Alexander smiled gently. "That girl is naught but a coquette. Surely you realized that? She flirts with any man who passes her way. And of course, there is also her penchant for titles. There was nothing in it for me. Forgive me." Kate forgave him with a new spate of tears.

"Well," she sniffled, trying to collect herself, for she abhorred the tyranny of tears, "I wish you had read my letter more carefully, for it would have told you not to bother following me."

"But will you forgive me?" Lord Alexander pursued, ignoring her last words.

"Forgive you? Oh, do go away," she exclaimed irritably. "What does it matter! Forgive you? Yes, all right! Now do let me go," and she felt his arms fall away and was more miserable than ever.

"Kate," Lord Alexander called softly as she turned aside. "Kate, listen to me. There is something in all this which matters to me greatly."

"Your masculine pride, no doubt," she whispered in a choked voice.

"In part," he smiled ruefully, "but it would be appreciated if you didn't hold it against me. You've been terribly provocative, you know." And suddenly her physical proximity was too powerful for him, and leaning forward, the Marquess caught her roughly back in his arms.

"You aren't going to hurt me?" Kate whispered, frightened by this unexpected move.

"Hurt you?" he echoed, stunned. "Is it possible that you could believe I would do such a thing? I love you, Kate." He threw caution to the winds. "Can you not have known that all this time?" And he lifted her chin gently and kissed her softly, but quite persuasively.

Kate was dumbfounded. Tears stung as she raised her fingers to her lips, trying to absorb his meaning. Perhaps this was some enormous hoax, she thought in panic, and froze at the very idea. "Let me go. You jest," she cried, unable to bear the thought of being toyed with.

"Kate." Lord Alexander frowned. "I meant what I said and would spend my life proving it, if only you would trust me." Then his lips came down roughly on hers, his final attempt to be understood where words had always failed him. It was a fierce, determined kiss which worked its magic, for Kate could no longer deny her own feelings.

"Tell me that you love me," she heard his whisper, his face buried in her hair. "I felt it just now, I'm sure I did, and have many years longed to hear you say so."

"Years?" Kate's eyes widened in disbelief.

"Years," Lord Alexander raised his head to smile at her incredulity. "Don't you know why I left England? I fell in love with you, one Christmas at Randomm. Do you not remember the night? I ran away, denying my discovery; have behaved abominably ever since and have much to be forgiven. But if you could find it in your heart . . . then I might regain my senses and make us both happy, instead of the proud wretches we are now. Kiss me, dear Kate, of your own volition, that I might know, once and for all, whether you really care."

Kate was stunned. He had finally said everything she had ever wanted to hear, and he spoke the truth when he cited her pride. But he had laid himself bare and now it was her turn. All he asked was a token of her avowal.

They stayed so for some moments and she saw the doubt flicker across his gray eyes. Another moment and he would release her and life would return to its old pattern. Every fiber in her body protested at such unhappiness and her heart pounded painfully; yet she hesitated.

Then his hands dropped from her shoulders, and Kate was truly free, and understood her hesitation. Lord Alexander leaned back wearily and closed his sad, tired eyes. Then suddenly he felt a featherlike touch on his lips. "I do love you, Alex," he heard Kate whisper, barely audible. "And I will marry you, come autumn, because I wish it. I wish it very much."

His eyes flew open, a great sigh escaped his lips. "Then we are finally in agreement, and at peace, my darling," and he held her quietly as they awaited the return of old John.

Let COVENTRY Give You
A Little Old-Fashioned Romance

☐ PERDITA   50173 $1.95
  by Joan Smith

☐ QUADRILLE   50174 $1.95
  by Marion Chesney

☐ HEIR TO ROWANLEA   50175 $1.95
  by Sally James

☐ PENNY WISE   50176 $1.95
  by Sarah Carlisle

☐ THE TANGLED WEB   50177 $1.95
  by Barbara Hazard

☐ MISS MOUSE   50178 $1.95
  by Mira Stables